"BURN, FERGUSON, BURN!"

Fun and Games Down at the Race Riots

By Blackface Rioter

A people united can build a tower to heaven.

A people divided destroy the world.

Or maybe we just all want to get off.

LET'S GET ONE THING STRAIGHT RIGHT OFF THE BAT. I'm
white as rice paper and I fucking hate it. White people are shit
at doing anything cool. I started noticing this around the mid-
90s. Everything cool had to do with black culture. White people
were listening to black music, dressing in fashion inspired by
black people–even talking like black people was considered
normal. I tried talking like black people, thinking I was cool, but
I'm sure I just sounded like an asshole. I covet black culture
because my culture is shit. We have the money, jobs, and all that
stuff, and that's cool. But after Y2K it was totally apparent to me
that: white people were so indoctrinated with keeping our rich,
safe, and predictable little lives stagnant, that we've lost our
ability to be dangerous. White people are born, raise kids, retire
on a fixed income, and die. I don't want a fixed income. I want
to bash teeth in. I want to scream 'fuck you' at authority. I want
to have sex without using a condom, without filling out a list of
past sexual partners, and fucking hell without swabbing my
junk with spermicidal lube. I want to throw a brick through a
window and hear the tinkling glass. I want what's happening in
Ferguson, Missouri. I want to riot.

 White people are shit at rioting. That doesn't mean that
white people don't ever riot. They do, quite a lot. They just suck
at it. White people riot over sports teams. Games. Right there
you know they really aren't going to put a lot of effort into what
they're doing. The Canucks winning the Stanley Cup might
make a few drunken Canadians burn a Honda Civic. Black

people rioting because they're getting killed by cops, that's where the juice is, I'll squeeze that fucking orange every day.

Loads of white people post memes on their Facebook pages ripping rioters for destroying property, ruining livelihoods, or just looking for a reason to burn the city they live in. Whenever I see these posts, all I can think of are fat, middle class, whites who've never had a run in with the law other than a speeding ticket. Not that I have a criminal record myself. I've gotten a few parking tickets and a fine from a parks warden once when I tried driving through the checkpoint at a state park without paying. That cop was a prick. Anyway, these people don't understand a good riot. Riots are awesome.

Throwing a fucking brick through a storefront window and watching the glass spider web in a hundred directions is the shit. Stealing an eighteen pack of Charmin toilet paper for the hell of it is the shit. Lighting up a cop car and watching twenty thousand tax payer dollars burn is the shit. Tossing a trash can filled with burning paper and watching the booted feet of a line of armored cops stomping through the fire to give you a tap with their nightstick is the shit. That's an adrenaline high that I've tasted and can't get enough of. The first time I tried it, though, I got the ever-loving shit kicked out of me.

Another thing you've got to know about me is that I'm kind of stupid. I'm not a fucking retard or anything. I just sometimes go at things head first and don't think about the consequences. That's probably why I work a shitty dish-washing job nights at a trendy Brazilian restaurant called Toro's. I told you that I'm not retarded. Like, I know it's kind of funny that they named the restaurant Toro's, because they speak Portuguese in Brazil and I think Toro is the Spanish word for bull. It could be the same in Portuguese. I don't know. I don't care enough to find out, but I'm not dumb enough *not* to wonder about it.

I know, you can add 'lazy' to the list of my personality traits. I didn't finish school. I dropped out junior year before they could kick me out. That's why I'm washing dishes. I don't think a high school diploma would have mattered much anyway. All the other guys who work the shit jobs in the back have high school diplomas and it didn't do them any better than me. In fact, I think I came out ahead, since I started working earlier than they did, so I made more money in the long run.

I make seven-twenty-five an hour rinsing off half eaten thirty-dollar-a-plate meals and then slamming a crate full of dirty dishes in a steaming hot power washer. Then I take the clean plates out, stack them up, and do it all over again. The restaurant is never slow, so I bust my ass every damn night. I've heard the customers usually drop seventy dollars a table- plus tip- for the slack ass wait staff, which I never see a damn dime of. I heard they were supposed to cut us in on the tips. I even mentioned it once. The waitress laughed at me like I just told the funniest fucking joke in the world. Anyway, this restaurant makes a shit load of cash and doesn't give any of us in the back any piece of that action. We bitch about it a lot, but we all know it's our own damn fault for being lazy and not going to college. Or, at the very least, be competent enough to be a member of the wait staff.

College. That's a fucking joke, now isn't it?

When the Ferguson riots hit I was all game. I took the night off of work. I called in sick and made myself sound like I was on my fucking death bed so the boss wasn't too sore at me. I don't take too many days off work because if I don't work I don't have enough to pay the rent on my shitty apartment. People always call the poor 'lazy', but it's usually the poor that have to work the hardest. I know I called myself 'lazy' just a little bit ago. Life is complicated and full of contradictions. Washing dishes isn't the same as building the fucking Chrysler Building, you know what I mean?

I drove over to about a mile away from where the shit was going down. I got out of my car and hoofed it over there where the action was. It wasn't hard to spot. The pitch black night sky was lit with an orange hue from burning buildings like the glow off a volcano. My nostrils flared as I breathed in the smoke. The yells and screams of people in a rage were almost louder than the sounds of sirens. I went alone. I wore black pants and a hoodie, not bothering to cover my face. I didn't expect to be arrested or even hassled by the cops. I figured my white face would be enough to keep me from harm. My walk turned into a jog as my blood pumped for some kind of destruction. Any kind. I wanted to fucking break something. I wanted to burn something. I got off on that shit.

Want to know something else about me? I haven't fucked in over six months. The last chick I banged was another dish washing slag at work. She was okay to look at, but she talked too damn much about shit I didn't care about. The only reason I gave her the time of day at all was because I knew she wanted to fuck. I knew this because she had been through most of the guys and even some of the girls who worked in the back. I heard she even fucked some of the people making the big money in the front. She didn't really talk to me at all before, but I guess I was next on her list of merry-go-round fucking.

I let her wag her jaw a bit, thinking about how nice it would be to shut her open maw with my dick. I was wrong. She never even sucked me off. I thought it was a slam dunk that she put dicks in her mouth because of all the people she screwed. Some chicks just aren't into that, I guess. Even though she wasn't going to suck my dick, she sure as shit wanted me to go downtown and lick her. I fell for that shit too. I was all done; she was all wet and had a couple orgasms already. I leaned back and took my pants off, pulled out my shit, and she just shook her head. What the fuck was I going to do? I have to admit that I was pretty ready to have my shit sucked, but it's not like I'm a rapist or anything. I wasn't going to force her to do it. Although I was pretty sore that she had me neck deep in her shit when she had no plans of her own to pay me back. Women. What the fuck can you do?

Anyway, she said some shit about not being able to cream well and that's why she needed me to lick her off or else she wouldn't get wet enough and it would hurt her too much to fuck. So I just fucked her for a bit, got off, and sent her on her way. That was over six months ago, like I said. I think she wanted to fuck again after that. She probably didn't want to seem like a one-night-stand whore or something. Maybe she was short on new dick to go after, but I ignored her. I found a better way to get off.

It happened first in Anaheim a couple years ago, a white man's riot, mostly. There were black people there, but they weren't on much of a race rampage. I drove a day and a night to be a part of the action. It happened when I tossed a brick through a window. I came in my pants. I didn't have a hard on before I tossed the brick, at least not one that I remember. I remember that fucking orgasm though. It was epic. It happened a lot that night too. The only problem was that I creamed myself so much that it looked like I pissed my pants, and the smell was awful, like I spent the night at a brothel banging twenty buck whores.

I fucked women since then, obviously, but it wasn't anywhere near as good as a riot jizz. So now I come (cum) prepared. I wear a jockstrap under my clothes without that plastic nut protector thing. I stuff that jock full of Kleenex so that it's nice and absorbent. This way I can cream my jeans all night and nothing shows through. All I have to do when I get home is take that sopping shit off and jump in the shower. I know creaming jeans is a girl's thing, but I think the phrase can be used for guys too. At least that's how I see it. Anyway, I was prepared.

I started jazzing myself up several blocks before I got into the shit. I was punching mailboxes over, kicking lawn ornaments around, all that kind of stuff. I spotted the first group of people a ways off and headed straight for them. Holy shit, things had gotten pretty intense before I even got there. There were the police. They were standing in a line in the street apart from the rioters. They were all decked out like soldiers. They had armor on and all that shit. I saw canisters fired into the crowd. Fucking tear gas. I love that shit. I've spent so much time in that shit that I don't hardly feel it anymore. My eyes tear up and all, but I don't have to shut them and run away like a whiney bitch.

I ran into the crowd of rioters and started screaming and jumping around like I was in a mosh pit. The other people seemed to take on my energy and started jumping around themselves. It was so tribal. Fucking awesome.

POWER. RAW POWER. That's how I feel when the crowd starts whooping into a frenzy. You can drive it, share in it, and fucking be it. Everyone is afraid of being shot, arrested, beat up, you name it. But there comes a time during a riot where all that shit goes on the back burner. Where it's not about your own personal safety anymore. It's about a cause.

Really, I don't give a shit what the cause is. My cause during a riot is all about me. It's what I need to get through the day. It's my drug. It's my high. I am high-octane motherfucker, motherfucker. The guys around me start smashing shit. A car window gets blown out by a brick. A storefront get smashed into. Twenty people jam inside to loot every last piece of merchandise. I see fires. Beautiful. I see a line of cops coming towards us. They are lined up like the Spartan 300. Their long, rectangular shields held side-by-side making a moving wall as they attempt to push the surging crowd back. In their other hand they hold batons which can easily strike out at any who

11

try and fight them. But I don't give a shit about that. I don't care for my own personal safety anymore. I am the devil on God's turf, and I want to burn this shit down. I charge the police. I feel the people run behind me. I see a black baton rise into the air and swing my own fist in a straight punch that I hope will break the cops face shield before the baton knocks me out.

My punch never landed. The nightstick didn't either. I took a shot on the left side of my face. It knocked me off my fucking feet. I've never been hit so hard in my life. I hit the concrete, bounced right off that shit so hard that I was sitting back up. I could feel blood coming down the side of my face. Then I could taste it, metallic and hot as tendrils of the wet stuff seeped into my mouth. I didn't have time to do much of anything because that was when the kicks started coming. I was kicked in my back and in the back of my head. It was fast and it hurt. Before I knew what had happened the beating stopped. I felt a crunch of boots on my right hand and saw the cops stepping over me, still in their phalanx line.

The fucking cops were protecting me.

I lay on the ground bleeding, trying to figure out what that must have looked like to them. I don't even know if the cops knew I was coming in to hurt them or to be saved by them. I don't know who took me out, but I know one thing. He was black. I know that because I was the only white guy in the middle of all that shit. I lay on the ground bleeding thinking about what a stupid fuck I was. I wanted what the black man had in his riots, but they sure as shit didn't want me. I wanted to raise hell, but instead I was seen as the enemy and was taken out.

Saved by the cops. Shit. I hoped this whole thing didn't end up on fucking Youtube or anything. Riot shit always goes viral and the last thing I needed was my boss seeing his sick employee running around causing mayhem. I would have a real hard time explaining that shit.

It was stupid of me to think that I could hang with the blacks during a riot that involved racist stuff. I thought that if I started up with them that they would see that I was on their side and they wouldn't care what color I was. This whole thing was about color, though. Black and white. I lay on the ground bleeding and I burned like a junkie that was too long out of a fix. Like I was given some of that weak shit from the hospital that is supposed to take you down off the high slowly. It was okay, but it wasn't enough. I was in a Mecca of pleasure and I could have none of it. I was a eunuch at a Roman orgy in the time of Cesar. My jock strap chafed against my junk. I wouldn't be creaming anything today.

I felt hands lift me off the ground and take me over to the sidewalk. White hands wiped my face and told me that I was going to be okay, and that they were going to get me an ambulance. As soon as my head cleared enough I lost those assholes and walked the long walk back to my car. Driving home was a fog of dark thoughts and blue balls. I got to my apartment complex and walked up the three flights of stairs to my room. I looked in the mirror and saw my face was a bloody mask. I could hardly recognize myself.

That's how I thought up the whole plan.

I took a long, red shower and cleaned up the best that I could. I superglued the gash in my head until it stopped bleeding and lay down on my bed to sleep. I was a long fucking time before I drifted off. I was going to call in sick the next day for sure.

I WENT TO WAL-MART TO BUY A RAZOR AND SHOE POLISH. The razor was an easy purchase. It's not like I don't know how to shave or anything. The shoe polish was different. I had no call to use the fucking stuff before and I didn't know what to get. Just like white skin isn't really white, black skin isn't really black. I ended up spending way more than I wanted to because I bought every shade they had. It came in these little black tins with a Kiwi on them. Not the fruit, the little bird mammal thing with legs and tiny wings from Australia. At least I think it's a called a Kiwi. Who gives a shit? Wal-Mart didn't have much in the line of shoe polish. I got everything they had, but it wasn't really that much. I got a tin of black, brown, and dark brown. I also picked up a pizza. I didn't spend much money on all that shit, but it was a lot to a poor-ass like me. I was hungry as fuck, but I knew I would have to make that one pizza last a couple days.

That's the trouble with being poor when you haven't always been poor. My mom and dad weren't rich by any stretch, but they kept food on the table and a roof over my head all right. I didn't think too much about it when I was small, but I think about it a lot now. When I lived with them I could eat a whole frozen pizza all by myself at one meal and not think anything of it. I like to eat a lot. They must have spent a fortune on food raising me. Like I said, I didn't think about it then, but I don't think kids do when they're just kids. They don't know the value of a dollar. I've matured a lot thanks to my job. You have to bend your ass over to make a dollar. If I ever had a kid I'm going to make sure he knows that money doesn't just fall out of the sky. I'll make him know that I worked forty-five minutes just to pay for that fucking frozen pizza, so he better be very fucking thankful that he gets to stuff his gob with it. Fucking brat.

I don't have a kid yet. This is a purely hypothetical situation. I like to think that I'm a planning type person. I want to know what kind of father I'm going to be.

So I check out at the counter and the checkout girl looks to be no older than sixteen. She should probably be at school, but I'm probably just judging a book by its cover. Maybe she's older than that. She's got a tattoo on her neck of a star, which is stupid because it pretty much guarantees her that she'll only be able to get a job at fucking Wal-Mart.

"This is a lot of Shoe Polish."

"It is."

"Do you have a lot of fancy shoes to be needing so much of it?"

"Maybe I do."

"You don't look like you do."

And there you go. Just as much as I was judging her while putting my purchases on the line, she was having a go with me. If I looked in the mirror I would probably judge myself much in the same way. I have shit clothes that I've worn the past couple days and a fucking glued up gash on my head. I don't look like a guy who needs a lot of shoe polish.

"Maybe I have a shoe fetish. My slovenly attire is only because I spend all my money on expensive shoes."

"Maybe you're just crazy."

"Is it customary to talk to the customers like this?"

"I wouldn't talk to you at all if you came to the line with a six pack and a box of Durex like a normal person."

"You don't think I'm a normal person?"

"Are you?"

"I like to think so."

"Twenty-three-ninety-seven."

"What?"

"You need to pay me."

"Oh."

I grab my wallet out of my back pocket and run my debit card. I'm not sure if there's enough on it. When the approved sign flashes across the computer screen and the receipt starts printing I'm a happy man.

"Thank you for shopping at Wal-Mart."

"Not likely I'll ever be back. The way you spoke to me."

"Yeah, right."

I think about taking the piss out of her right then and there. I could raise my voice and cause a scene. Maybe even get her fired, if I shout loud enough, but I can see the glazed look in her eyes like she's lost all interest in me. I lost interest too. It's no use tearing into someone who doesn't give the slightest fuck about you. The small hit of conflict would only make me itchy for another go at civil unrest. I wish I was hooked on heroin or meth or something rather than the specific type of violent anarchy that I am. If all I wanted was heroin there were a million different places I could get it.

I knew people that use the shit. When you work shit jobs like I do there is always someone there who's using. You can always spot them. They've got black and red circles under their eyes and they just go through the motions of work like they're on some kind of death sentence. You always have to repeat yourself to them because they never hear you the first time. It's fucking annoying, but nobody gives them too much hassle about it. They're never around that long anyway. They're on the fucking brink.

They even talk about their drug habit like it's no big deal. It's like they don't care anymore that they're doing something that could put them in prison or get them fired. They know they're fucked, but all they talk about is getting clean and laying off the junk. The only time they are really serious about getting off drugs is when they are starting to come down from their latest high. They're feeling only a little mellow and a little sick. It's enough to get a bit of remorse when all the good part of taking a hit leaves your body, but you haven't really hit the hard part of the sickness yet. Really they're just hanging onto the job until they get so desperate for the drugs that they start stealing. When you're stealing for your habit you don't show up for work anymore.

Anyway, drugs are easy to get. Riots are not.

I get back to my apartment and go upstairs to work out my outfit for tonight. There's bound to be another week of rioting in Ferguson at least and I don't want to miss out on one second of that action. It's not often that I get to do this so close to home. It's like a delivery service right to my door. I don't usually plan out what I'm going to wear to a riot. So picking out an outfit makes me feel kind of gay.

LET ME GIVE THOSE OF US WHO AREN'T FROM AMERICA A QUICK REVIEW OF HISTORY. America is the greatest country in all the world. We police the shit out of everybody, and if you don't like it we will nuke the shit out of you. We have always been like this. Our history is full of violence of the worst kind. Wait just a fucking minute? Your country was built on violence too? Big fucking deal. The funny thing about us Americans is that we think that our violence is somewhat different and perhaps maybe even a little bit more special than the violent histories of everybody else. We don't like to read about other countries' history because it's old and boring. America is new and awesome. America is interested in America. It's not that we don't throw another country a bone, you know, help them out from time to time, but every action is of personal interest. Even if it's something stupid like digging a small country out of an earthquake to get us a little good press.

We just sign them a fucking check.

Race relations in our country are shit. Of course, this is pretty much true in every country except for fucking Sweden, but I bet it's there too. I've never been to Sweden, so I don't really know. What happened here in America was there were these indigenous people here who loved nature and all that shit and called each other 'Little Bear' or 'Silent Arrow' or other odd names. They were, of course, the Native Americans. The main thing you need to know about the Native Americans was that they were pussies. They don't like to think of themselves as pussies, but that's exactly what they were and are. They were a bunch of pussies waiting to be fucked and getting fucked is exactly what happened to them.

A white guy named Christopher Columbus landed on the Eastern shore and basically said, "See all this shit here? This is all fucking mine now." In school you learn different. Like he was some sort of explorer and they show you pictures of him looking all gallant and shit. The dude had no other plans except to conquer, pillage, and settle America and that's just what he did. Columbus bitch slapped the Indians (That's what he called them. Dumb shit thought he landed in India). This leads me to point one of why America is the greatest country in the world. Mercy. Americans are always sugar coating our violence like it's not really what it is. We placate while we rape. There was really no reason to allow ANY of the Native Americans to live, but we did, and that's mercy. God Bless America.

Columbus started the slave trade when he couldn't find gold. The dumbass thought he would just be picking gold off the ground in large chunks or some shit. He had to provide something else of value and that's why the fucking slave trade was booming all over the fucking place in America. Of course, that's not to say that Americans invented slavery. That would be like saying I invented my own dick. Slavery was rampant everywhere in every fucking country and not just across color lines. Whites enslaved whites. Blacks enslaved blacks. Browns enslaved browns. Yellow enslaved yellow. People are assholes. If someone can make good money by kidnapping a person and selling them off – there's going to be a long fucking line of people wanting to take the job. Sure there were people against slavery, but it wasn't as many of them as there are now. Freedom may be a word that we Americans like to throw around currently, but it wasn't always so. The white boys were the ones kicking ass here. Everybody else got their ass kicked. That's just how it was.

I'm going to skip forward a bunch by saying that Americans got civilized and did away with slavery. White people killed each other off by the fucking bucket loads to do it, but in the end we were civilized. Sort of. We didn't drink from the same drinking fountains for a bit, but that got sorted out too. You'll notice I'm only talking about the whites and blacks and not the Native Americans anymore. Those pussies are sitting in 'reservations' subsidized in such a way that they don't have to do shit, but drink and die. It's a nice way to finish off the genocide. Slow, but nice.

Anyway, white people and black people have a lot of problems now. White people think that black people should be over the whole slavery thing because it happened such a long time ago. However, there are generations of black people still alive that experienced the hardship and horrors of segregation firsthand and still feel the sting of it. White people think the

20

system is fair for everyone. Black people don't. Black people think that cops and authority are targeted against them. White people feel victimized by black crime. Black people think they understand white culture – they don't. White people think they understand black culture – they don't. It's one big fucking mess with violence boiling right below the surface.

None of this is ever going to get better. Anyone who truly believes that people of other skin colors are ever going to get along is a dumbass. Even if we were all the same color we would still find some reason to kill the shit out of each. In Africa, blacks were killing blacks based on the shape of their nose or some shit. I saw it on movie once. In Thailand they've had this seventy year genocide going on with the same color killing the same color. I guess I'm trying to say that it doesn't matter what we look like, we're still going to find reasons to kill each other.

Black and white, though, that's as simple as black and white. The Native Americans weren't a problem anymore since they were dead or put on reservations which are basically life sentences, paid up deadbeat time. The whites didn't kill the blacks and so when everyone was declared free, or whatever, you had all these people of different races who hated the shit out of each other.

This is perfect for riots.

Anyway, a couple of the beefs are real between the races and some aren't. It's fucking true that whites are the victim of black violence a whole fucking lot. It's not true that blacks are always killed by police. More white people are gunned down by the cops and not the blacks. Why don't the whites riot? It's easy.

Cops hassle black people all the fucking time. If you're black in America, the cops are going to be on your shit. What I don't get are the fucking Asians in America. Cops are barely killing them. Maybe we should all just learn some fucking Kung Fu so that when the cops are about to execute you, you just run up the side of a building like fucking Jackie Chan.

We've had four blacks killed by cops in a short span of time that have made big news. The score is that two of them deserved it. Two of them didn't. They were murdered by the cops. The Civil Rights Movement latched onto one of those assholes who totally fucking deserved it and polarized the races even more. If they only waited until one of the legit cop murders, then there would have been a whole lot of people holding hands and singing Kum-by-ya. Lucky for me, they didn't.

And don't go talking to me about the fucking French being the best at this uprising shit. I have to admit that the revolution shit they've done a lot in their culture is impressive, but it's not my thing. Revolution equals responsibility and Lord knows I don't want any of that shit. I just want to fuck shit up.

HOLY SHIT. All that bringing everyone up to speed took a lot longer than I thought. I have to haul ass or I'm going to miss the good stuff. I like to get to a riot for the ramping up. Going late would be like jerking off and then putting your dick into a girl right when you cum. It's just not as satisfying, and I plan on getting mighty satisfied tonight. At first I tried smearing the black shoe polish all over my face, but that shit stung the cut on my forehead.

I washed off the area as best I could, but I had to deal with the sting for a while. Looking in the mirror told me that my plan was total shit. I looked like a guy who had been working under a Ford F150 all day, not black. I took some scissors and cut off my hair as close as I could and then shaved my pate bald right down to the skin. I bandaged the cut and then smeared the polish all over my head again. This time was better, but I had to go back and shave my fucking eyebrows and polish over those. I also polished my lips because they were the wrong fucking shade.

I looked in the mirror again. Pathetic.

I once read this book called, 'Black Like Me.' It's about this guy who went black to get a taste of what their culture was really like. He did all this skin tanning stuff and had a lot of help in the process. Here I am trying to do the same thing in fifteen minutes. Now it's dark outside and I can already hear the news talking about civil unrest that's happening and I'm not a part of it. Time for the fish to cut the fucking bait. I put on some shoes, jeans, a black t-shirt, and a black hoodie. I rub more shoe polish on my face and all around my head until I can't see a speck of white skin showing. I tie a black bandana around the lower half of my face and put on a pair of sunglasses. You can barely see any part of my skin. I put the hood up and I think, in the dark, I can pass for black. There's only one fucking way to find out. Before I leave the apartment, I stuff a bunch of Kleenex into my jock to catch cum.

It's time to go and have some fun.

I TOSS A GARBAGE CAN FULL OF BURNING TRASH THROUGH THE BUSTED OUT WINDSHIELD OF A COP CAR AND I JUICE MY JOCK. I bend double with ecstasy, feeling people pound me on the back, laughing and whooping. I turn away from the fire. That shit is so hot that it's making the shoe polish run down my face and burn my eyes. I don't wipe them clean. I can't afford to take off the sunglasses. I stand tall and begin to run after a crowd of young men who are running full tilt away from an oncoming horde of cops. And Jesus, these cops mean business. They've been kicking our asses just as much as we have been dishing it out. They look like fucking soldiers. I guess the National Guard was called out right away, but I don't think these guys are the National Guard. I think they're just cops.

They aren't dressed like cops. They're wearing riot gear, with the plastic shields and whatnot, but they've got this shit on that looks like Batman's armor and boots that look like Robocop's. They aren't fucking around either. Gas canisters are flying all over the damn place. Rubber bullets are being shot. It's made things a little fucked up. The protesters are really fucking pissed off too. They're attacking firefighters and shit. I'm not into that shit too much. I'll throw stuff at the police if they're all geared out. I don't think it will hurt them too much under all that armor, but I don't want to hurt the firefighters. If we start taking them down then all of us are going into the paddy wagons lickity-split. Can't have that.

I skirt down grand with a wooden baseball bat that I picked up off the ground a couple blocks ago. It's packed with people, but they aren't too worked up. I work my way down the block taking out storefront windows. I don't stop to do a really fine job of it. I just jog along going smash, smash, smash. I cross some cigar bar where they've got three big guys standing out front looking mean. They've got a pit-bull with them and they're all carrying bats. I decide to play baseball with them. I run straight at them and hit the dog on the side of the head with my bat. The dog falls sideways and quivers like he's having a seizure. A split-second later I reverse movements and take out the dog handler with a swing that catches him on the chin. Then I sprint. Nobody tries to stop me. The other two guys give chase, but they're fat and they can't keep up. I start laughing. The last sounds I hear from them are yelled racial slurs. I slow down my jog and go back to taking out shop windows. Smash. Smash. Smash.

Ahead is a pack of blacks looting a gas station and I head over there. There are a couple small fires in the parking lot, but those are getting stamped out. Stupid assholes that started the fires are getting chewed out. People are running around the gas station taking everything from toilet paper to Slurpee. A couple of guys are inside trying to beat open the ATM with bricks. Fat lot of good that shit is going to do them. I remember the pizza I bought earlier and how it's supposed to last me a couple of days until payday. I'm going to need to grab some food.

I skip passed the people fighting over goods. Blacks and whites both trying to grab chips and candy and other worthless shit. I can't live on chips and candy. I've tried and it makes me feel fucking sick. The alcohol is almost all gone as well. Not surprising. I don't need any of that shit either. I make a grab of a couple loaves of bread and some cans of soup and head out. It's going to mean a trip to my car and back but at least I'll have food for a couple more days. Then I can concentrate on the really fun stuff without worrying over my empty stomach. Much to my surprise, I'm stopped by a news reporter on my way out. I look down, trying to mask my face as much as possible.

"Sir, why are you looting?"

"Everyone else is."

"What did you take?"

"Food. Cans of soup and bread."

"Why?"

"I can't concentrate on getting off when I have hunger pangs."

The reporter says something else, but I am deeply uncomfortable in front of the cameras and shit so I take off. I stow the food in my car and check my disguise. It still looked pretty fucking good if I do say so myself. Then I run back into the fray. The good shit isn't hard to find. I follow the booming sound of tear gas and see police walking in a line, pushing back rioters, making small traps as they pick up the rowdier ones and arrest them on the spot. I picked up a brick as I'm getting close and let fly at the nearest cop from the side. It hits that fucker right in the side of the helmet, knocking him sideways. I pick up another brick and let fly. It catches a shield, doing no damage, but I've disrupted their ranks enough that the blacks start pushing the breaking line back.

The armored car must be somewhere else, keeping the firemen safe or something, because all we have ahead of us are these military cop guys. There aren't any gas canisters firing off. It's just us and the cops. The cops know that they're fucked. We know the cops are fucked. This is great. They're spread too thin and now we can have a little fun. They start a quick-step retreat and we just start throwing shit at them. Anything we can find. Rocks, bricks, bottles, trash, anything that can catch air, we toss it. The cops are blocking the flying debris with their shields and are backpedaling, but I can see that they are pissed off.

One cop stops just blocking and start slamming the incoming projectiles with his shield like it's an offensive weapon. I can see his mouth moving. He's yelling, but I can hear anything over my own voice hurling swear words, threats, and basically just screaming whatever I want. The cop stops moving back and stands there in front of his brother cops yelling and smashing items thrown at him. A couple cops break rank and try to bring him back into line. All three of them were soon on the ground bleeding. As soon as that cop stopped staying with his buddies, I picked up speed and slammed into his shield while the others tried to grab him. That cop went down and I started taking an ass beating, but then a bunch of black guys jumped the cops around me. I climbed up on the cop's chest and started banging his head into the street. I think I was dry humping him too, because I could feel my hips slamming into his utility belt.

He tried bucking me off, but this wasn't my first rodeo. Giddy-yup little doggies.

My lust for violence overpowered my lust for dry humping. Lurching to my feet, giddy with bliss, I ran forward and pushed ahead of the blacks running so wild that I attacked the cops with my hands in the air, like I was an Orangutan about to bring down my powerful arms in skull cracking hammer fists. Well I'm not a fucking monkey, and my arms are pretty spindly, to tell you the truth. I never got to hit the cops anyway, because I was hit by a fucking Taser which dropped me like an asshole. I think I jizzed my pants again on the way down. I like the rough shit. Charge me. Light me up. Make me whole.

"Get up, baby."

"I'm not done. More."

"Oh, you're done. I think you should come home with me."

"I can't."

"I will help you up, but I can't carry you."

She put my arm around her shoulder and helped me to my feet. She was a heavy broad, but pretty. She was also black, which was terrifying. I don't have any black friends. There are a few of them at the place where I work, but I don't think I can count them as friends. I heard someone say that you can't count a person as a friend unless you've had dinner at their house and they've had dinner at yours. It sounded right at the time, but I guess on paper the statement looks a little dumb. I don't really have any friends if you go by that logic. I don't think I've even touched a black person before. I think I might have given one a high five once, but I wasn't the one who initiated it and I didn't have enough time to think about it before I slapped his hand. I don't even remember what that felt like really.

She was doughy, but her skin was smooth. Looking at black skin that close made me think that my hypothesis about black skin being tougher was right. Black skin is like a shell over the white skin underneath, giving black people a very small extra layer of skin for protection. It's also the reason why there are more successful black people in sports like football and boxing. They are a more durable ethnicity.

I was kind of pissed off that I couldn't riot anymore. I wasn't sure if there would be many more days like today before everyone cooled off, but I was more mesmerized with being handled by a black person to care much. She ended up walking me all the way to my car, holding onto me tightly the whole way. When we got to my car she helped me into the driver's seat and moved my groceries to the back. To my horror, she sat down in the passenger's seat.

"What are you doing?"

"You're taking me to your house. I need to look after you."

"You can't come to my house."

"You just drive. You don't have to worry about anything."

I drove.

She smelled different than anyone I have ever known. Her hair smelled like many different things and I don't really know if the smell was pleasing or not. She reached over and touched me on the arm. I pulled my hood over a bit more to hide my face.

"People looking for you?"

"I don't think so."

"You were very brave tonight."

"I was just trying to get off."

"You can't be peaceful forever. You can only be pushed so far until you start pushing back."

"I like rioting."

"I know what you mean. There's so much anger in the street. Sometimes it feels good to release the anger."

This was the longest conversation that I ever had with a black person and I think it was going okay. I don't really know what to say to black people. Do I have to apologize for the whole slavery thing? I've never owned a slave, but my forefathers did. I'm pretty sure about that. She thinks I'm black, so I don't think I should bring it up. There were black people who had slaves. I wondered if black people kept track of these things in, like, a log or something so that they knew which black people owned slaves so that they could apologize to each other when they met. I wondered if black slave owners had to pay reparations to slaves. Maybe they were the smart ones. They got to own slaves *and* they got reparations. That's a double-dipped chip.

"What are you thinking about?"

"Chips."

"I can cook up some of this food for us when we get to your apartment. I'm hungry too."

"The pizza is mine. You can have some soup."

We got to my apartment. I parked the car on the street and we went inside. She must not have her apartment on the third floor like mine, because she was huffing and puffing by the time we got all the way up the stairs. I unlocked the door and we went inside. I was a little embarrassed by my apartment. It was clean-ish. It's not like I was expecting company, so I didn't dust or anything. She didn't seem to mind. She went right to the kitchen and began putting the food away and going through the drawers to find plates and a can opener. I went into the bathroom and checked my outfit. I looked pretty much the same except I had a little blood on my face and I was dirtier. I decided not to add any shoe polish because I thought the smell would give it away. I left my hood up, bandana over my face and the sunglasses on, of course.

I guess you're wondering why I let the black woman in my house. To tell you the truth, I don't know. I guess I thought she wouldn't really come home with me. She doesn't even know me. How many people just go to someone's house that they don't know? Maybe it's a culture thing and all black people go to each other's houses. White people don't do that. They shoot people for just barging in. I'm also a little afraid to ask her to just leave. What if she says no? *Then* what do I do?

I leave the bathroom to see her waiting by a plateful of soup. I don't own any bowls. My pizza has been torn into fourths and piled on my plate in a gooey mess.

"I microwaved it. The stove doesn't work."

"Okay."

I sit down to eat. She reaches over to try and take my sunglasses off, but I stop her hands. She clasps my hands in hers and looks into my eyes. Or at least she thinks she's looking into my eyes. With the shades on, she can't really be so sure I'm looking at her, which I am. It's just worth it to make the point, I guess.

"You can relax around me."

"I want to leave my sunglasses on."

"I understand. It's hard to trust anybody anymore. Even someone of your own color."

"I want to eat."

I take my hands out of hers and begin eating my pizza with a fork and knife. She finishes her soup before I'm even half done with my pizza. I'm beginning to feel full because I don't really eat much, so I just plop a quarter of the pizza into her bowl. She thanks me and eats up what I gave her. I guess she doesn't mind pizza dipped in soup remnants.

I finished off my pizza, eating every last bite until it was gone. My stomach felt stretched to the nines, but I didn't want to leave any and let her eat my food. I knew I would be going hungry again, so I wanted to make sure that I had a full gut. You've got to take these things when they come to you. I got up and went to my bedroom. She followed. I told her that I was going to go to sleep and she made a move to join me in bed. I told her that she would have to sleep on the couch if she was staying. She nodded and told me that she understood, then went back into the other room and left me alone.

I could hear the television blaring away a minute after she left. She had the news on. I went into the bathroom and took a long shower, washing myself as clean as I could. I walked back into my room with my pajamas already on and a towel over my head, making as if I was drying my hair. She didn't even look at me as I walked past. I went into the bedroom and locked the door. I didn't even know my bedroom door had a lock on it until today. I guess I never felt the need to lock the door in my own fucking house. It was weird, having a stranger in the next room, but I couldn't bring myself to shoo her off. I was hoping she would leave the next morning. I was hoping even more that she wouldn't steal or eat all of my food.

I got into bed and was just going to sleep when I heard a knock on my door.

"You're famous."

"I'm trying to sleep. I have to work tomorrow."

I heard her footsteps recede and then the sound of couch springs squeaking as she sat down. The walls of my apartment are paper fucking thin and you can hear everything.

"Holy shit, you're famous!"

I shut my eyes and went to sleep.

I WAKE UP TO MY ALARM BLARING FROM ACROSS THE ROOM. I don't keep the fucking thing next to my head because I would just end up flinging the bastard into a wall and going back to sleep. I have to get up to shut off the infernal noise and I've found that by the time I get out of bed and walk across the room I'm calm and awake.

I unlock the door and go to the bathroom and get dressed, shoe polish on skin, with bandana around my face and sunglasses. It looks fucking ridiculous, but what can I do? Going out of the bathroom, the black chick is still there lying down on my fucking couch and snoring. I guess thinking she would split was just a fucking dream. It's shit having someone in your apartment. For the first time in a long time I feel myself stepping quietly, trying not to wake her. What the fuck is that all about? People shouldn't have to live with one another. I don't think anyone should have to. All it does is fuck you up from what you would normally do. I don't like to think about other people. Never have. The black woman wakes up anyway. She sits up and adjusts her hair and tits. She looks like shit, but everyone does when they wake up. She doesn't seem to think anything about looking like shit because she just starts talking to me.

"Get over here."

"I'm going to get some food and then go to work."

"You're going to come over here first."

"Why?"

"Paying for the room."

I go over to her, not really sure why. Why the fuck should I have to listen to her? I think it's because she's black and I'm not comfortable with that. It's my fucking apartment and I should be able to tell her to fuck off. Maybe it's because of slavery or racism or something. Like I owe her something. But that thought is too stupid to even think about. I go over and she reaches out and pulls down my pants and boxers in one fluid motion. She screams and I clap my hand over her mouth. She bites down hard and it's all I can do to yank my hand back before she rips off a piece of my flesh. Now I have fucking bite marks on my hand, but I have to worry about this fucking black chick screaming before I can give myself first aid and some antibiotic ointment. I've heard that human bites are the worst, and I don't know if there is an ethnic difference to how you can be infected by a human bite. Are black bites worse than white ones? I think Mexican bites are probably the worst, but I couldn't tell you why right off the top of my head. It just feels right.

"You're white!"

"No. I'm black."

"Your dick is small and white! You're white!"

"I have that Michael Jackson thing. I'm black."

"What fucking Michael Jackson thing? Oh…I see."

"You are the one who yanked down my fucking pants. What did you expect to see?"

"A black dick. That's what I expected to see. Your balls are all small like a child's."

I looked down, and sure enough, my balls were no bigger than a rotten walnut. I can't say that I'm very surprised by it because I've been cumming the shit out of myself every day for a while.

"Does the Michael Jackson thing affect your dick?"

"No. Just my skin."

"Okay. Bring it back over here."

"I don't want you to suck my dick. I take care of that myself."

"You?"

"Not like that. I take care of sex differently."

"Okay…You know you're fucking famous."

"Why?"

"You're all over the news."

The television is still on. I don't even pull up my pants even though I can see she is still looking at my dick like it's the most interesting thing in the world. She even reaches out to touch it, and I just barely back away in time. This chick is crazy. Even crazier, I am on the news. I'm all over the news. There's video of me throwing the burning trash can, tackling cops, smashing windows, and then my interview with the reporter. Holy shit.

"I've got myself a famous man here."

I walk back over to her and allow her to do what she wants, although I don't expect to get hard, I do. It's not from her generous movements down below. It's what I'm seeing on the television. Fire. Violence. People getting fucking off by being animals. Looting. Breaking. I fucking love that shit. I can't get enough of it. I want to fuck off of work again and go back to Ferguson, but I know nothing it going to be happening there. There's going to be a bunch of people cleaning up and protesting in nice little packs and all that shit. That's not my fucking scene. I want the violence so much that I start pumping my hips thinking that my dick is smashing through a burning brick wall. The broken bricks are falling all around me. I dance in a sea of broken glass. I swim along on top of a throng bent on vengeance and destruction. I cum, but it's not much of one. The black chick looks pleased enough though, and lies back down on the couch.

"I'll see you tonight."

"Don't eat all my food."

I pull up my pants and quickly go down the stairs and to my car. I put the pedal to the metal so that I'm not late for work. Before I leave the car I wipe the polish off my face with rubbing alcohol and water. I know I'll smell like shit, but lots of the people I work with smell like booze so I don't think I will stand out too much. I hate the day shift anyway. It's all the work that the lazy bastards didn't do the night before. All the food is caked on the dishes and shit and there's usually something we have to do in the front like dusting and other rinky-dink shit.

I go into the restaurant and clock in. My boss doesn't say shit to me. He just nods and goes back to gawking at the television. Useless fucker doesn't ever do any real work, but I am glad that he isn't giving me shit about being sick and missing work. I couldn't miss too much work anyway. I have to pay my fucking rent and missing two days really puts a crunch in my ass.

I'm passing by the television and I see they're watching the news. I'm on it. Shit.

"SIR, WHY ARE YOU LOOTING?"

"Everyone else is."

"What did you take?"

"Food. Cans of soup and bread."

"Why?"

37

"I can't concentrate on getting off when I have hunger pangs."

Cut to a big shot looking black man with silver in his hair and a two-thousand dollar suit.

"What we have here is a much broader issue than just race relations or police violence against blacks. This man is just one among thousands of blacks who don't have enough to eat. We do not condone violence of any kind. But there are times when violence is necessary. Who would not commit acts of violence to feed his family? Why are people starving in this great nation of ours? There is no reason for this type of atrocity. It is becoming more apparent now, more than any time in our history, that the black man is marginalized through industrial racism. Just because he's not being led about in chains anymore, doesn't mean that he doesn't wear them still. This man was brave enough to put himself before the cameras and tell it like it is. He is a victim who will no longer be punished just because he is black. End of story."

Cut to a big shot looking white man with silver in his hair and a two-thousand dollar suit.

"What we have here is nothing more than a man taking advantage of a situation to loot, pillage, and steal. There is no higher purpose to what this man is doing. He is acting like an animal, over what? Slavery? That ended a hundred and fifty years ago. Maybe if he put a little more time and effort into getting an education and achieving a job then he wouldn't be running rampant through the streets and ruining good people's livelihoods. This is just a thug acting like a thug and it must be

stopped. This has nothing to do with race. This has everything to do with opportunity. This man is nothing but a hoodlum. End of story."

Cut to edited video of me messing up shit. I feel myself getting hard watching the violence but I'm able to tear myself away and get back to my station before I run out of the store and start throwing bricks through windows.

The dishes are piled high in the sink and I fight the urge to scream epithets about the night crew. This shit should have been cleaned up easily by them if they weren't so fucking lazy. Most of the time I work nights and I don't leave the back this fucked up for them. Maybe they think I don't have enough to do during the day when the restaurant is quiet, but I'm pretty sure they're just fucking lazy fucks. I start rinsing off the dishes with water so hot that it nearly scalds my skin, but it's the only way to get the dried grime off last night's gorging. I work so hard and fast that when my boss actually takes the time to come to the back and chew me out, he doesn't. He even asks me how I'm doing and thanks me for my hard work. You're welcome, dude.

I slow down when another cleaner 'accidently' slams my hand in the dishwashing door. He doesn't do it too hard, but it fucking hurts and I get the message loud and clear. Slow the fuck down. The restaurant could be as clean as crystal, but then that would be the expectation, not the exception. Working slow and easy gets us all through work without busting our ass too much for the shit pay we're getting. The restaurant gets reasonably clean. I would even eat here, although I can't afford too. No sense busting our ass over pennies. Double our pay and this place would be as clean as the bosses' asshole after he gets a ten dollar rim job from the crackheads downtown. It's just something I heard he does. Every man needs a hobby.

After a couple hours I get a clap on the shoulder from the guy who bruised my hand.

"Let's take a break and smoke."

We go out the back door and into a small fenced in area. The ground is a concrete slab that's dotted with old gum and cigarette butts. Stacked off to one side are plastic crates that get sent back with the food delivery guy on Mondays at drop-off. The area leads to a gate where we keep the trash bin. There's always homeless people rooting through the garbage trying to find discards they can eat. Some of the other staff hate them and chase them off, but I don't give a shit. At least they're not trying to grab McDonald's garbage or some other shitty place. These homeless have some class at least. I'm not the only one who works here who has a heart for them. The poor have to stick together. There's this one guy who scrapes the leftover food on one bin that he leaves near the top so they don't have to dig too much to find the good stuff. He will even leave a little note saying if something is rotten and they shouldn't eat it. The people usually eat it anyway. The poor have stomachs of iron.

My co-worker takes out two cigarettes, lights them both, and hands me one. It's a peace offering and I take it even though the cigarette being in his mouth makes me feel a little gay putting it in my own.

"Sorry I slammed your hand."

"It's fine. Next time just say something."

"I did. You were in fucking la-la land or something."

"Yeah."

"I was also trying to tell you that you smell pretty bad. Normally I wouldn't say shit, but it's pretty awful."

"I haven't washed my clothes in a while."

"It's worse than B.O. It's like you fucked a rotten ham all night or something."

"I had sex this morning with a black woman. She gave me head."

"No way!"

"Yeah. She's at my place."

"You're living with a black person?"

"I guess so. It's only been one night."

"You have to tell me. What's it like being with a black woman? Are their clits bigger than a white girls? Because they have to take all that big black dick all the time."

"I don't know."

"I heard they are shitty at giving blowjobs. Is that true?"

"I don't know. It was hard for me to get off."

"You're kind of shitty to talk to. Getting details is like pulling teeth with you, man."

"I'm not sure of what to tell you."

"I've heard that black women are always okay with anything. Did you do anything freaky with her?"

"I don't know. I think it's kind of the same as having sex with a white girl."

"You are fucking hopeless. What a waste of interracial fucking."

"What?"

"Never mind."

He left and went back into the restaurant. I barely smoked my cigarette, so I stay out and take my time with it, getting as much smoke into my lungs as I possibly can.

WORK WAS PRETTY MUCH A BLUR FOR THE REST OF THE DAY. I slowed down a bit so I wouldn't piss anyone else off, but I did get a lot more done than I usually do in a shift. The evening crew will be pleased because they won't have anything more pressing to do than smoke cigarettes until it gets busy. I walked up to my apartment and listened at the door. I heard soft singing coming from inside. That black chick was still here I guessed. A part of me thought that she would have left because she was bored or something, but that wasn't the case. I wondered if she had nowhere else to go. Maybe I picked up a homeless person. She smells different, but not bad like homeless people do. I open the door and walk inside.

She sees me and screams.

I clamped my hand over her mouth and ignored her teeth clamping down into my palm. I listened but I heard no one. I'm sure the neighbors heard the scream, the walls being so paper fucking thin and all, but people in transitional housing are used to the odd scream every now and then. Nobody leaves their place to knock on my door. I don't even hear anyone moving, so I'm pretty sure no one gave enough of a fuck to call the cops.

"I'm going to take my hand away. Don't scream."

"Who are you?"

"I fucking live here."

"With the other guy?"

Oh, shit. I forgot I was supposed to be black. No wonder this chick screamed.

"There is no other guy. I'm the same guy. I'm not a black guy. I'm white."

"I thought you had that Michael Jackson stuff."

"I lied."

"I sucked off a white man?"

"You did."

Repulsion is a weak commentary about the look on her face. I won't waste words to describe it.

"You're all over the fucking news."

"I know."

"What are you going to do?"

I hadn't thought about that before. There being a couple layers to what I was going to do, I mean. What I wanted to do was blackface myself up, wait for nightfall, and go hitting the streets like I did last night. I didn't think I would have to *do* anything. What the hell was I supposed to do? I wanted to be there and do what everybody else was doing, fucking shit up. I knew what I didn't want to do and that was stay home and sit this one out. No fucking way that was going to happen.

"I'm going out."

"The police will be looking for you. Well, not really you, but the guy that's on the television. They're making you out to be some sort of poster child for all this shit. You're not even black!"

"I just wanted to fit in. I tried it before as myself and got beat up."

"Well what the fuck did you think was going to happen?"

"I thought that the black people would think that I was on their side and they would leave me alone."

"You're a fucking crazy person. What the fuck am I going to do with you?"

"Pay for the room?"

"Are you trying to be funny?"

"No."

"You can get that thought out of your head right fucking now. Do you know what my people will do to you if they find out that you aren't black?"

"Kill me?"

"You're fucking right they will."

"I just want to riot."

"Go find some white boys to do it with then."

"It's not the same thing."

"You're damn right it's not. You are well out of your league on this one, you crazy ass fool. You have no idea what you've gotten yourself into. Stay home."

"I can't do that."

"Well, if you're going out you have to play the part in full. You have to be the poster child."

"I just want to break windows and shit."

"Well, go on then. I don't know what to do with you."

"Are you coming?"

"Hell, no. Now that I know I've sucked off a white man, I'm going to have to do a little soul searching. I could have you charged for rape."

"Are you?"

"Get the hell out of here."

I did. It was weird having her talk to me in this way. It wasn't even her apartment. I didn't even know her name. Even though we had gotten very familiar with each other, it still didn't feel right for me to just kick her out. Doesn't even fucking matter. The best thing about the incident was that it killed daylight and I could get my shit together and head out to the fray. I went into the bathroom and shaved my head again. There was a bit of stubble that had grown since last night. I put the shoe polish on and my outfit, stuffed my pants full of Kleenex and headed out the door.

"Bye."

She gave me a half wave as if I barely existed and went back to watching television. I hoped she didn't eat all my food.

I KNOW I'M GOING TO BE RECOGNIZED. My face was on signs held by the peaceful protesters. My words were being called out in chants by hundreds of voices. I came in on a side street, cutting through an alleyway, and headed into the rowdier groups of people. I was an anonymous black man for a few blissful minutes as I screamed and ran up and down the street trying to get the blacks to start really fucking shit up. The attitude was much more subdued than last night, which really pissed me off. The thing that bothers me most about my hobby is that you only get a couple good nights of fun before people calm down.

Luckily I had Illinois blacks coming to town for one reason only; loot and mayhem. There was some press about the people of Ferguson not really being the problem. It was blacks from the Illinois border driving over and really putting the boots to the cops. This was partially true, but there were plenty of locals in the middle of the riots as well. There was no real way they could blame Illinois for all the hateful shit that was going down, but it was relevant. Illinois blacks are a real pain in the ass to Missouri blacks. I fucking love the Illinois blacks because they keep things violent for a while longer. Some whites are even blaming all the black violence on the Illinois blacks, refusing to believe that the Missouri blacks had anything to do with it. It's an 'our blacks are nicer than your blacks' kind of thing. Interesting.

The cops aren't playing around anymore, if you could call the ass-whoopings, arrests, and tear gas launching practices they were using before 'playing'. They are cracking down on any type of violence, swarming around rabble rousers and tossing them into armored paddy wagons. There are many stand-offs in front of the police station and businesses. Protestors on one side of the street and the cops on the other. I'm getting antsy because everyone seems to be protesting and not rioting. This infringes on my cause of getting off. I go to different groups, walking around, trying to find the spark that will lead to fire. There is a palpable feel of violence, fear, and anger on both sides. I feel like a shark that smells blood in the water, but can't find the source. Even though I see my shrouded face on protestor signs, and I know the cops are looking for me, nobody seems to recognize me. I don't understand any of this shit and I'm getting really confused. All of a sudden I find myself surrounded by cops and realize that I've been dry-humping a parking meter.

"You're under arrest."

"Parking meters always consent to my love!"

Rough hands grab me. I try and comply with directions, but there are too many voices shouting at me and I don't know which ones to listen to. I get punched in the stomach and a stick laid across the back of my thighs. I try to kneel like the cops are commanding me to, but even when I take my full weight off my feet cop arms are holding me up. I get thumped a couple more times, cuffed, and tossed into the back of the paddy wagon.

A couple arms pull me to my feet and help me onto one of the long bench seats that line the side of the walls. Not everyone is cuffed. It's pretty dark in the back of the police wagon. I see a bunch of black faces staring back into mine.

"We know who you are. We are with you, brother."

A hand pounds on the wall that separates drivers and the arrested.

"Get ready for a rough ride to the station, fuckers!"

The small lights went out in the back of the van and I don't think it was an accident. The paddy wagon lurches out into the street and zig-zags along the pavement, sending everyone in the back tumbling together in a pile of cursing angry people. I take a knee to the face and the person leans the limb down into my grill, hurting and suffocating me. I can't stand back up. My legs are pinned under other bodies and my cuffed arms are useless. Screaming is hard when you have no air, but I manage enough to finally become noticed. The asshole that has been crushing my face finally gets off and I'm helped up to a sitting position. I kick my legs until they are again free. Someone punches me in the back of the head, but I don't give a fuck. I don't know who these fucking people are and I'm not going to die in the back of a fucking police van for anybody. Hands reach down to stop me from kicking as we are hurled about. I notice that I'm the only one trying to hurt the others and I calm down. A black face appears right in front of mine. His eyes grow wide.

"Holy shit, there's a white guy in here."

"Kill that motherfucker."

I begin to kick again. This time, for my life. I'm getting punched and choked at the same time. I don't know where the shots are coming from.

"They're killing me. I'm the one that's on the television and they're killing me."

"Get your hands off of him!"

"He's a white dude!"

"Fuck you, Uncle Tom motherfucker."

I have no idea what this means. I think I might be dying as the car runs over a rough patch of road and the fingers tighten around my neck. Others are beginning to join the small fight at the back of the van, attacking the men that are pinning me down and hitting me. The fingers release from my throat and I take a sharp inhale of air into lungs that seemed to forget how to work. I begin kicking again, at anyone and everything in the van at once. I can't see shit in front of me. Everyone is now punching, kicking, scratching, and biting. Well, maybe I'm the only one biting, but my arms are fucking behind my back. What the fuck else am I supposed to do?

I find a throat and rip it out with my teeth. I can feel my erect penis rub against my pants leg. I ejaculate a fountain of sperm into my jock as I am bathed in blood. The blood only makes the others fight harder. A couple of them have knives. I know this because one enters my leg in the shin and others scream to the stabbers to stop.

This shit is so fucking awesome I can hardly contain myself. It's a blind fucking free-for-all-clusterfuck of a brawl- and I'm right in the middle of it. Several times the group tries to stop, but I keep kicking, biting, and head-butting them into action again. Sometimes I scream for help. Other times I search out to the ones still breathing and stomp on their necks until they stop moving.

Let's get one fucking thing straight. I am not a murderer. I don't wake up and look for people to kill. I don't fantasize about offing people in horribly twisted ways. I'm just a guy who loves violence. I've been waiting for this shit all day and I haven't found what I'm looking for. Now I'm all juiced up when the shit hits the fan and I can't control myself. I have to get off and I'm fucking going to. Half the people in this car were trying to kill me or protect me. I don't give a shit either way. I've got a big hard-on and stomping boots and neither are going to stop pumping until I run out of juice.

All the while the paddy wagon is rampaging through quiet streets as it tries to fuck us all up on its way to the station. The van slams to a stop and the bodies fly forward. I smack face first into a pile of bloody meat. I bite into the closest flesh I can find and get a couple mouthfuls down before the back doors open. A group of cops face the interior, which looks like the floor of an abattoir before it's hosed down for the night.

"Holy shit!"

"What the fuck?"

"Get them out of there!"

I spit out a mouthful of skin as cops pull me out of the van. One of them takes a quick look at me, his eyes go wide as he sees my face without the bandana or shades. He knows who I am. He slips a cloth bag over my head and hauls me inside, calling for a couple cops to help with the escort. I can still hear the ones left at the van talking as I'm being led away.

"They're all fucking dead in there."

"Holy shit. This city is going to fucking burn after this."

"What the fuck did you do?"

"I didn't do anything. We arrested them and drove them to the station."

"Were they fucking alive when you arrested them? Were you videotaped?"

I WAIT FOR THE COPS TO BOOK ME. To tell you the truth, I don't really know what that all entails. I've never been arrested before. I assume that they're going to take my picture and fingerprints and shit. I'll get a change of clothes and have to squat and cough while naked to show that I'm not hiding anything up my ass, which I'm not. I'm not gay.

None of that shit happens. I get taken to a room, sat down in a chair, and the hood ripped off my face. It's the same type of room that you see in all those cop shows. The walls are painted white, and they're dirty. Old ceiling tiles, some water-stained and sagging, are above. There is one-way glass where I'm pretty sure people are watching me. There's a camera in the upper corner of the room near the door. The cop sits down across the table from me and folds his hands. I can't stop looking at myself in the one-way glass. I'm covered with blood all down my front. I look like a fucking serial killer. Maybe I *am* a serial killer. I'm not in shock. I've never looked so fucking cool in my life. I'm awesome! The cop taps on the table and I turn my head to face him.

"I know who you are."

"Yeah?"

"You're the guy on the television that all the blacks are getting so jazzed about."

"Yeah."

"You're white."

"Yeah."

I really don't know what I'm supposed to say to this fucking cop. The 'Yeahs' keep popping out of my mouth, and I don't really know how to stop them. The cop seems a little annoyed with me and stops talking for a second. Maybe he isn't annoyed, just considering what the fuck is in front of him.

"Does anyone know you're white?"

"There's this black chick at my house who knows I'm white. People at my job know I'm white."

"Why are you doing this?"

"I like to riot. I like fucking shit up."

"Did you kill all those people in the car?"

"Some of them, I think. I'm not sure if I killed all of them, but some of them I'm pretty sure I did."

"What happened in the car? Why did you kill them?"

"Fucking self-defense. I didn't go into the car thinking I was going to kill them, but you have to look out for yourself, no? A black found out that I was white and tried to kill me. Then some of the others thought I was black and tried to save me. I really like stomping on people, and the space was enclosed, so it was hard for me to just stomp someone a little bit and move on. It's not my fault that I couldn't move on. I just kept stomping."

"Just stomping?"

I flicked my tongue across my teeth and found a sliver of skin still stuck in my maw. I spit it out onto the table. It was a black strip of skin with a patch of curly hair attached. Fucking gross.

"It was fucking self-defense."

"There's someone on the way to meet you. I thought you might be of interest to him, so we skipped general pop and brought you somewhere private. He'll be here soon."

"Okay."

The cop looks me over for a bit and then shrugs, gets up, and leaves the room. I wish he had taken the bit of skin with him because it's grossing me out. That's some sick shit right there.

"SORRY ABOUT THAT, SUSAN, BUT WE HAVE BREAKING NEWS FROM THE FERGUSON RIOTS. We have just gotten word that seven people who had been arrested by the police during last night's riots arrived at the police station dead. The police have not issued a statement, but the chief has promised one later this evening. Videos of the people being arrested have been submitted to our station by several listeners. As you can see, the people that were arrested were alive. This leaves the unanswered question of what happened to them from the time they were arrested to the time they got to the police station. We have Todd on the street, speaking with locals about the situation."

Cut to Todd, a tired looking man with a News4 windbreaker jacket on. He is surrounded by a group of protestors. He is being bumped and jostled by the unruly crowd as he tries to speak to them.

"What do you think happened to those people?"

"It's not what I think. It's what I know. These people were taken alive, and then killed on the way. The cops have declared open season on black people. Black lives matter. We are fed up with our people dying due to cop violence and brutality. We will not tolerate this any longer. Cops have guns. We do too. For every black life lost, we will repay ten-fold! "

"Sir, are you threatening to kill members of the police?"

"We are only standing up for our own lives. The police are killing us with abandon and that will be stopped one way or another. Not one more black life will be lost to police brutality without repayment in full."

Cut back to the station.

"Thank you for that report, Todd. Be careful out there. With us now is Steven Jacobson, head member of the resolution party response team. Mr. Jacobson, your group has been offering services to business and homeowners who have been affected by these riots, but you've had criticism because you only offer aid to Caucasians. Can you explain?"

"I would be more than happy to, but first, I would like to say that the resolution party response team is very happy to come and support clean-up efforts. So far, we have pledged over ten thousand dollars. We are a privately funded group, so our monies are spent at the discretion of the management team."

"Do you exclude ethnic groups?"

"We choose who we support in the clean-up and rebuilding efforts. We also offer monies for a relocation program for people to move out of certain areas. Yes, we support white people, but only white people who meet our requirements. They must be Christian, law-abiding, Nation-loving folk. Which really are the foundation of the white race. We are a civilized country which has fallen into a Marxist/Communist instilled way of thinking that could even be called a movement against our civilized Christian society. Racism against whites is at an all-time high. Blacks only want *freedom from law and order. We have to fight against people from third world nations (whom our founding fathers tried unsuccessfully to deport) who are intrinsically unable to adapt to functional society. White people, like our agency, refuse the indoctrination of self-loathing and choose to stick together.*

"Okay...um...Let's go take another look at our weather! Back to you, Susan!"

SO I'M SITTING AT THE TABLE, COVERED IN GORE THAT'S ALL FUCKING DRIED UP ON ME NOW, STARING AT THIS LITTLE PIECE OF BLACK SKIN ON THE TABLE IN FRONT OF ME, WHEN THIS GUY COMES IN THE ROOM. He's wearing orange, and I'm pretty sure he's not a guard. Dude has tattoos on most of the skin I can see, except for his face. He's blonde and older. At least older than me, but I don't really know for sure. He's kind of wrinkly around the eyes and shit. Guy sits down across from me and folds his hands looking me over.

"What?"

"We know who you are. Do you know who I am?"

"No."

"I am a part of a certain group that is very interested in you and your story."

Dude pulls his shirt sleeve up and shows me a swastika tattoo. This is pretty exciting for me. I've never really met a real live Klan member before. At least not that I know of, but you never really know. I could have Klan members all around me outside of prison and not really know it. Well, not I, since I live in a black neighborhood, but you know what I mean.

"Holy shit! You're a Nazi!"

"Not really, no. But I can see the iconography isn't lost on you. Normally we wouldn't work with you because you've violated some core beliefs of ours, but you've given us an interesting chance which we would be silly not to risk."

"What are you talking about? When will I get a shower?"

"Hopefully soon. Let me tell you something straight. We own this part of the prison. It belongs to whites. Since you're here, you belong to us. You owe us, or else your ass would have been in gen pop and you would have been beaten and had a train run on you by now."

"What's a 'train'?"

"Shut the fuck up or I'll have my guys pump you full of white semen instead of black."

"Okay."

"We're going to book you quietly, get you cleaned up, and then have you placed in solitary for a day. You're charges will be dropped and you'll be sent home. What I need you to do when you get home is stay there. I'll have some money ready for you when you go. You won't dress up and paint your face black again. I need that guy lost forever."

"No more rioting?"

"None."

"No more fucking up shit?"

"Nope. Not unless you want to cut chopped into fourths and dropped in a dumpster."

"Oh. How will I get off?"

"Not my problem."

The guy stood up, took another look at me, and left the room. I didn't like the way he looked at me. It was like he thought I was crazy or some shit. I didn't know what I was going to do. It was good that I was going to get out of prison. I was hungry and I knew I had food at home, but what was I going to do if I couldn't riot? I don't think the guy even wanted me to go to my job, and then I would surely get fired. He told me that he was going to give me money, but how much? I didn't think I would be getting into trouble with white people, but I guess you never really know who you're going to piss off in this life. That fuck can threaten me all he wants, but I'm going to get off. When I get out of here I'm going back on the streets. White people can be a real pain in the ass.

THE NAZI GUY WAS RIGHT. I was released less than twenty-four hours after going to prison. I was booked, washed up, and given an orange jumpsuit that I wore for only a little bit until they came and got me to go home. I tried finding out what the whole 'train' thing was about, but nobody would tell me. Some cops laughed when I asked them, and some told me that I shouldn't be asking about that or else I would get one. Prison is fucked up, but I guess when you're behind bars you get to obsessing about stupid shit like transportation.

I walked all the way back to my apartment, maybe a hundred blocks or so. I planned on getting my car back that night, but it was probably towed already and fuck if I had enough money to get it out. That white Nazi guy told me he was going to give me some money. He did, but it was only a hundred and twenty bucks. That's a lot of money to me, but it won't cover my rent if I lose my job, and it's a far cry less than what a towing charge will cost me.

I get to the apartment and go inside. The place is a fucking pigsty. I think I told you that I'm not the cleanest person ever, but I'm not a fucking slob. That black chick made a fucking mess of my place. I don't know how she did it. I wasn't gone that long, and when I left she was lying down on my couch watching television and coming back she's in the same damn place. How can someone mess shit up when they haven't moved? Mysteries abound.

"You ate all my food?"

"There's a can of soup left. I saved it for you, honey."

"Are you…Are you leaving soon?"

"Do you want me to go? I thought we had a good thing going here."

"Well…"

"It's about the whole 'white dick' thing, isn't it? Don't you worry, boo. I've done a lot of soul searching, praying, and talking to my friends about it and I'm okay with sucking a little white dick for a while. It might even be good for my shit. Black dick stretches it all out and shit, making it look kind of like a sleeping basset hound. Maybe that shit will shrink back a bit if I only pound it with a little dick for a while."

"I don't really like to have sex."

"I know, honey. You have revolution on the mind. You're not thinking about simple things right now, and that's hard on a man. I have an opportunity for you which might get your mind right. I've been in touch with some of the brothers who are leading the black movement against cops and white oppression. I didn't tell them much. Just that I know you and that you are alive and in my care."

"I'm in your care? This is my fucking apartment."

"Hush, honey. They are very interested in meeting you."

"No fucking way."

"I didn't tell them that you're a white man. You don't need to worry about me ratting you out. I would be in just as much trouble as you if that happened. You don't have to meet them. I didn't think that you would want to. I *did* set up an engagement for you."

"What kind of engagement?"

"A speaking one. They want you to speak to the black movement leadership and the people. Tons of my people are going to turn out to hear you move them with words to help the cause."

"I don't really speak well in front of people, especially black ones. They don't have a lot of facial fluctuation. At least in my doings with them."

"Look, just don't say shit like that and you'll be fine."

"Like what?"

"Don't be a fool. Just speak out against the white man. I'm sure you've heard enough speeches and news reels that you won't make yourself look like a fool."

"I don't think I can."

"It's a thousand dollars for ten minutes of your time."

"I think I can."

"That's good, honey. That's good. There's something else I want to talk to you about."

"Okay, as long as it doesn't have to do with public speaking in front of black people."

"It doesn't. You'll be speaking in front of white people. It's the same deal except you'll get an extra grand. White people have more money so I put the pinch on them."

"That's racist."

"That's business, honey."

"So now I'm a public speaker? I'm Henry Rollins now? You're lucky that I need this fucking money or else I would never do something like this. I don't even talk to myself in the bathroom mirror. I don't even talk to my mom, and Lord knows she's been wanting to talk to me for years. Every six months she gives me a call and I let the machine pick up. It's suffocating!"

"You just need to relax and be yourself. Or should I say — yourselves."

"That's not fucking funny."

"But you're going to do it, aren't you?"

"Yes."

"Good."

THAT NIGHT, WASHING DISHES FUCKING SUCKED. When you think about a time in the near future where all you have to do is talk for a bit and then get paid some real money for it, a minimum wage slog just doesn't do it for you anymore. I don't like people any, but if celebrity makes money fall into your hands, then you can put me on that fucking track. It's not like people know my real face anyway. At least not the black one.

I'm well into my night of work and it's getting fucking hot as hell. You get into a rhythm at my job. It starts off slow and time doesn't seem to go anywhere, then you get into a flow of scrub, tray, and slam into washer, take out, put away and back again. The time starts to fly and you don't even fucking know it. It's like fucking Zen happening right in front of you. I love it when work flies by, but there's a shit part about it too. Your life is just flying by. I spend eight to ten hours a night on my fucking feet slamming dishware. What kind of fucking life is that? That's shit. It's like the time I spend at work isn't time that I truly exist. Sometimes my flow is interrupted with this nugget of thought and then the whole thing comes crashing down. I get all depressed and time seems to stand still. This job fucking sucks.

I'm sweating like a motherfucker. The hot rinse and the steam off the washer is drenching me. People complain about how my shirt sticks to me all over, but I tell them that if they want to have a go at what I'm doing and stay fresh as a daisy, they are more than welcome to try. People always complain about shit they know nothing about. Washing dishes is sweaty work. That's all there is to it.

My fucking boss comes over to me and taps me on the shoulder. I think I'm going to catch hell for a spotty fork or some shit, but he doesn't have that pinched look he usually gets before he rips my ass.

"There's some people to see you. Why don't you take a break and go out to the dining hall. They're at table seven."

You could have hit me in the face with a ballpeen hammer and I would have been less surprised. My boss is a total asshole. This guy never gives me a break. I wiped my hands on a sodden towel and walked through the kitchen door into the dining hall. I knew right away why my boss was so fucking freaked out. The table was full of fucking Nazis. I know they're not called Nazis now. They're the white knights of the something or other, but they're still Nazis. At least they believe in all the same dogma bullshit. I don't like to judge. Everyone needs a hobby. I'm still going to refer to them as Nazis. Makes shit that much simpler for me.

The table was full of two types of Nazis. There are the clean cut Nazis that you wouldn't ever know they were Nazis if you saw them walking down the street. They're dressed nicely. You can't see any hate tattoos on them. Their hair is clean-cut and short, but you wouldn't be able to tell by just their fucking hair if they were Nazis or not. These are the people you see every day. The other fuckers, now *they* were straight up Nazi bastards. They had swastika tattoos on their necks and wrists. They wore wife-beater shirts and fucking Capri looking pants. I don't know what the fuck they were. They didn't go all the way down to the ankle, but they were too fucking long to be shorts. I guess it doesn't matter much. These guys were the soldiers of the bunch. They were the crazies that did all the criminal shit that the nicely dressed ones told them to do. Ten fucking guys in all. The wait staff pushed three tables together for them. I went up to them and just fucking stood there.

"Have a seat. We ordered dinner. I got you the stuffed chicken."

"I hate the stuffed chicken."

Holy shit, I need a fucking filter. Any sane person would have thanked them.

"Sorry. The chicken is fine."

"Good. Wine?"

"No, thanks."

The tattooed up guys were drinking beer or hard liquor. The dressed up ones were quaffing wine. It must be in the Nazi rules or something.

"What do you do here?"

"I wash dishes."

"You like doing that? You like being a servant?"

"I fucking hate it, but it's a job."

"We could fix something up for you with one of our people. It would suit you a lot better than this place."

"Okay."

I didn't know what to say to the guy. I had ten pairs of eyes on me and I didn't like any of them. The way there were looking at me, I didn't know if they wanted to fight me or fuck me.

"I'm sure you're wondering why we're here."

"Yeah."

"Well, I told you to lay low and now I hear you're speaking at a black event, *as well* as a white one. How does that work?"

"My girlfriend set that up. I had nothing to do with it. The money is good and I need it."

"You're going to cancel the events. We don't want you speaking at either one of them. If you do, your body will be found in a dumpster. Do you understand me?"

"I do."

"Just wash dishes and lay low, like I told you to do before. I'm serious. Don't try and fuck me over. We will be in contact soon."

Waiters arrived with our food. They put it down with a flourish and refilled wine glasses and brought fresh beers. I picked up my fork to eat, but noticed that the Nazis were just sitting there looking at me.

"What?"

"You are dismissed. Fuck off."

The Tattooed up Nazi on my left took my plate and dumped the food onto his. I rose and went back to my dishes. My boss didn't bother me for the rest of the evening.

I FEEL PRETTY DAMN GOOD AS I'M SLAMMING DISHES INTO THE SINK TO RINSE. I get the graveyard shift tonight, which means I get to keep busy until the shit really starts hitting the fan on the streets. I don't have to go through all the effort of whipping people into a frenzy. The people are going to have to take that on for themselves. I'll be hitting the streets swinging. I fucking hate foreplay anyway. I just like to slam it in there and jizz all over the fucking place. I don't play around. This is about me. The fucking populace could be a package of bologna with a hole cut in the center waiting for me to jam my dick into it. Not that I've done that. That shit is sick. Okay, I've done it a couple of times, but I can't be the only one out there. Put a wad of bologna in the microwave for ten seconds and it's about the same consistency as a ready clit. It's just as fucking smelly as one too. Women are gross.

"Put down that shit."

I turned to see three of my co-workers glaring down at me. I say down because these fuckers are fucking tall, big, and black as fucking night. They are standing too fucking close to me. I've got my back to the counter and these fucking dudes are surrounding me. I don't know what to fucking do. I've barely said five words to these guys since we've started working together.

"We have a message for you from your white brothers."

"Who?"

"The skinheads that came by to see you earlier."

"What is the message?"

"You fuck him over. We fuck you over."

The guy gave me a quick look up and down and bit his lower lip. Shit. Holy, shit, these guys were going to try and rape me. There's three of them, so I'm pretty sure they're going to get that shit done. Three big blacks versus one little white guy isn't really a competition. At least I wasn't a virgin in taking a dick up the ass. I'm not gay or anything. Don't get any ideas. I just totally passed out drunk at a party once and woke up to a guy sucking me off.

It actually didn't feel too bad, so I let the guy keep going as I slipped off back into unconsciousness. When I woke up again the guy was fucking me in the ass. That was crossing the line. It wasn't even the same guy. There were other guys in the room, so I was pretty worried that they had run a gangbang on me while I was passed out. I got that guy to pull out of my ass, got my clothes back on, and limped home. I couldn't fucking sit down comfortably for two weeks after. I don't feel too bad about it though. Those guys get off by ass fucking drunk men. If I didn't want to get ass-fucked I should have taken it easy on the booze. It's not like the experience really hurt me any.

That is, unless they gave me AIDS or something. Maybe I should have that shit checked out. If I had AIDS then I would have to find someone else who has AIDS to have sex with. It's the responsible thing to do. I only like to fuck after rioting, and people with AIDS are all thin and sick and shit. I don't think it's been studied, but people who are all wasted from auto-immune disease don't riot. They just don't have the fucking energy.

"I might have AIDS, you know? You might want to think twice about what you're about to do."

"Nice try."

"I'm telling you the truth."

"You can't get AIDS from fucking someone in the ass."

"Of course you can! How do you suppose all these gay men get it? Do they fuck each other in the crook of the elbow or something?"

"Turn around."

I turned around. It's not that I was going to enjoy what was about to happen to me, but when you're obviously going to be fucked, you might as well let it happen. This is just my opinion. If you fight back you will still get fucked, and get beat up in the process. It might even get you killed. My advice for all you men out there is to take the fucking and live to fight another day. It won't be long before doctors and specialists are sticking things up your ass every few months or so looking for cancer polyps or some other shit. You might as well get used to things getting jammed up your ass when you're young. You don't want to go into ass-jammings when you're all old, dried up, and puckered out. There isn't enough lube in the world to make that a smooth experience.

Also, what if you're fucking gay and you don't know it? When the doctor puts his finger in your ass, a yelp of pleasure might come unbidden from your lips. That would be fucking embarrassing. If you knew you were gay and going to enjoy the cancer test, you could make yourself ready so that the doctor wouldn't know you were getting off. These are things that any normal man takes into account. The gays have to be careful, especially the ones who don't know they're gay yet.

Now don't you all get to thinking that I'm gay. I'm not. Since I was molested by other men, I have developed a safety system for myself. I don't mind gays wanting to get off. I just don't want them getting off on me. I've used my system of anal defense twice before and it's worked every time. The first thing that I do is shit myself.

"Holy fuck! This guy shit himself!"

The middle black had yanked my pants down only to come face to face with a pile of thick wet shit, clumped in the seat of my tighty-whiteys. The three were quiet for a moment, except for gagging noises. I just stayed where I was. I don't want to risk a beating. I have rioting plans tonight.

"I'm not fucking that shitty ass."

"We have to fuck him. We got paid."

"No fucking way."

"What do you think will happen to us if we don't?"

"We could just say we did."

"We are fucking this guy."

"You go fucking first then."

"Not all shitty like he is. We're next to the fucking sink. Make him clean himself up first."

Crap. This was definitely a hole in my defense plan. I never thought I would be raped at work, so being next to a commercial grade sanitation system didn't cross my mind. I stripped off my boots, socks, and pants. I turned the water on and dunked my own ass in the sink. My ass was filthy and soon the whole back room smelled like shit. I had to drain the sink three fucking times before I had all the shit off of me. The thought crossed my mind that no matter how much soap, bleach, or fucking steam cleaning happens in that sink, it will still have been the receptacle of a lot of human shit. My shit. I'm sure it can be sanitized, but in my mind, it's now a toilet. I will never eat here again. All I can think about is how many people eat here a night. What if there are still microbes of my shit in the sink that transfer to the dishes when I clean them? My shit microbes would be in thousands of people in a month.

I retch.

"Don't even think about puking on yourself. I'm not staying here all night while you stall. Let's get this shit over with. Turn around and bend over."

I turned around and bent over. I told you before that I have a self-defense system for protecting my ass. In reality there are only two components to this system. The shitting myself thing had worked so well that I didn't really think I would need anything else. It was shit myself and if that didn't work I would go to the last resort maneuver.

I would use the taint razor.

When I was just a child I went camping with my Uncle. They had these shitty showers at the campground that were really only open stalls with a shower curtain cover. The curtain was up so high that I was worried that everyone could see my wanger. My Uncle and I could speak from one stall to the next.

"Don't forget to wash your taint!"

"What's a taint?"

"Your Daddy never told you what a taint is? You must have the filthiest taint ever."

"What is it?"

"A taint is that little section of skin between your balls and your ass. You know, it 'taint' your balls and it 'taint' your ass. It's your taint. Take a moment and find it down there."

I reached between my legs and got my hand behind my balls. I could feel a small ridge of skin there.

"Did you find it?"

"I think so."

"Give it a good scrubbing. That taint of yours probably has never been washed since you fell out of your mother's crack."

My Uncle helped me to both learn about my body and confuse me at the same time. I was now aware of the taint. I was now under the assumption that babies were born from their mother's assholes. This made more sense to me since the asshole looked a lot larger than the vagina. I still have a hard time believing that babies fit out of that damn little hole.

Anyway, the taint razor is exactly what you might think it is. Every day I tape a small blade to my taint. I've been doing it for years in case this type of situation arises. When I first learned about my taint from my Uncle, the information was quickly forgotten. The taint is pretty much useless on its own. However, since becoming an adult, I've come to think of it as a perfect hiding place that doesn't involve an orifice. One of the black guys, I don't know which one, lubed up his dick with dish soap and jammed it into my ass. Holy shit, did that hurt, but I welcomed the pain. Not because I'm gay, but because I needed my enemy close. Having your enemies dick shoved up your ass is pretty close, I reckon. A person does a lot of flailing while they're being raped, so my movements didn't distract the black guys all that much. I ripped the tape free from my taint and in one swift backwards motion with my hand, I chopped the black guy's dick off.

70

I tried to turn around and yell in triumph, but I had a huge severed dick up my ass, and that puts a hamper on your movements more than I thought it would. The guys whose dick I cut off was screaming. I felt blood drip down my legs as it oozed out of the dick in my ass. I turned my head around to face my attackers.

"Who else wants a piece of this ass?"

The blacks grabbed their bleeding friend and dragged him out the back door. I would have assumed that if the hurt one was of sound mind, he would have asked for his dick before he left. I'm pretty sure they can sew that shit back on. Too late now.

I make a hunchbacked shuffling walk over to the sommelier's section and took one of his corkscrews. I carefully twisted the corkscrew in the severed dick in my asshole. That thing made a champagne cork pop when I pulled it free. I thought about leaving the dick on the corkscrew and leaving that on the sommeliers desk. I hate that fucking guy. He's a prick, so I thought I would leave a prick for a prick. That would have been stupid though. Can't leave things like severed dicks around and still expect to have a job the next day. It hurt to walk around after being raped, but I managed to clean everything up. I finished off my work for the evening and went home. Just another day at the salt mines.

I UNLOCKED THE DOOR TO MY APARTMENT AND WENT INSIDE. The black chick was lying down on the couch watching the morning news. One of these days I'm going to come home and see her actually standing up.

"How was work, honey?"

"I was raped and washed dishes. It sucked."

"That's nice."

"I've been thinking about that speaking engagements you've set up for me. I can't do them. If I do then the skinheads will send black people to rape me."

"That doesn't make sense."

"Tell me about it."

"I've already told them that you're on board to speak. You can't back out now. Hush up now. The President is on."

I turned my attention to the dipshit in a suit on the television.

"We interrupt this story with a special message from the President of the United States. We are filming live from the White house. Chip?"

"Yes, thanks. This is Chip Roverson reporting live from the White House. The President is just about to…He is starting now.

The President, an older black man with deep crow's feet wrinkles that marked his face even when he wasn't smiling, stood behind a podium that bore the presidential seal. To his right the Vice President, a white man much older looking than the president, stood with his arms crossed and brow furrowed.

"My fellow Americans, the world is watching the ongoing situation in Ferguson, MO. We must band together as a country in the name of peace. We need to rise beyond the

destruction of racism. We must hold our police accountable for their actions, as well as supporting the ninety-nine percent of the police force that keep us and our families safe. As an African American man, the people's struggles on the street hit close to home. If I had children, they would want to join in this fight. It is my wish and hope that cooler heads prevail."

"I would like to jump in here, Mr. President." The Vice President steps to the side of the President and moves the microphone over. "I would like to say that peace is the only way we can come together and sort this issue out appropriately. I would like to say that if I had children, they would want to join in this fight as well. Just on the other side."

"Excuse me, Mr. Vice President. I hope you're not insinuating that I'm taking a side in this volatile situation."

"Excuse me, Mr. President. I think that's exactly what you're doing."

"Is there something wrong with what I said? As the president I can represent a man of peace for my people."

"The insinuation is that your people are the ones getting a hard time and that you approve of what they're doing. I don't see the comment as being peaceful at all. It's incisive."

"Yet you reiterated what I just said. Sounds to me like you're throwing your hat in with your ethnicity."

"Just balancing the scales."

"If they were balanced before, which would be a hard argument on your end."

"You'll all have to excuse the vice president. The situation in the middle of our country has him upset, as it has us all, no *doubt. I'm sure if he could be reflective on his words he would have chosen them differently."*

"No, I wouldn't, and you don't have to speak for me."

The Vice President gives the President a little shove. I can feel the tension from across the country, watching these two on my television. It's about to go down. The President waves off the secret service, who look like they don't know what to do about this. When the President's men step forward, the Vice President's men do the same. A wave from the commander-in-chief makes them pause.

"You think you can just lay hands on me and there won't be any repercussions? You're just along for the ride here, bub. I'm sure that being the Vice President has made you pretty tired, going to all those elementary school open houses or whatever it is that you do to fill your time."

The President gives the Vice President a little shove. The two men glare at each other.

"The only reason I took the job as the Vice President is because I thought that the American people would assassinate a black president. It's a no-brainer that I expected to take your seat."

"Why don't you come over here and try it?"

The Vice President steps in on the President. The President slaps the Vice President hard across the face. The Veep swings back, but both men get tackled by the Secret Service, who drag the kicking and screaming men away from each other and out separate doors. The room erupts in cheers and fighting from the reporters. The camera quickly cuts back to the newsroom and the two stunned anchors.

"Well… What do you think of that speech?"

"I think it was pretty fucked up. I'm going home."

"I'm with you."

The anchors get up from their desks and leave the table empty. The camera rolls on.

I look down at the black chick on the couch. She's fondling my flaccid cock. I move away. She rolls her eyes and lays back down. I wonder why in the hell she thought that I was in the mood to fuck. I'm never in the mood to fuck. Watching other people get off with violence doesn't do much for me. It's like porn. I don't fucking get how watching other people fuck makes any difference. After all, you're not the one doing the fucking. It's some other dude that's getting off.

I could try and get it up for the black chick, but it would really only be for her benefit. She's the one who doesn't live here. I think that she thinks that giving me sex is what's keeping her here. That's really not what I want. Maybe she could clean up the place or get a job and pay the rent or something. That would be something to think about. I know that what she's doing isn't really doing much for me. With the exception of getting me these paid gigs and all.

Maybe she's the one who needs sex to get off. She can't be getting what she needs just sitting on the couch and doing a whole lot of fucking nothing. She had to do something to get me those speaking gigs. Maybe she's getting off the couch and doing shit while I'm not here. I don't know. Black people sleep all damn day mostly. At least that's what I observe. Maybe there's a few black go-getters out there that get up and do shit like the white people do. Actually, this isn't all that honest. There are plenty of fucking trailer parks filled with white people who don't do shit. White people and black people are both lazy – except for their hatred of each other. There isn't any laziness about that shit.

"You ready to go speak to the white folk?

Fuck it.

"Sure. Let's go.

"I PRESENT YOU WITH THE MAN WHO HAS TAKEN THE FOREFRONT OF THE BATTLE FOR OUR RACE. He stands, and we stand with him, united. Together, we will restore law-and-order, and protect our creed and our race from decimation by blacks."

Applause. I walk up to the podium and immediately wish that I had dressed better. The place is full of white people starched out in their Sunday best. I have a feeling that I'm in the wrong place until I look to the back and see what must be the huddled masses behind the suit parade. I see the stars and bars of the South displayed proudly. I see Christian flags hung along the sides of the aisles. I see people that could be mistaken for a trailer park convention. These are supposed to be my people, and in many ways I guess they are.

"Hi. I'm here today because I was asked to speak my mind about the black race. I understand that they are very bad and we are gathered together because they are very bad. First, how can you identify a black person? It's easy. Their skin is much darker than ours. Sometimes they try and trick you by having skin that isn't really all that black. Do not be misled. Look at their hair. Is it tight and curly? Black. Are the palms of their hands and feet a much lighter shade than the rest of them? Black. Are they Mexican or Hispanic? Black. Why? I don't know, but you cannot trust a black man. Especially if it's a Hispanic one. Asians? They get a pass. They don't get into much trouble so we don't have to worry about them yet. As our motto goes, 'Worry about the darkies now, we'll take care of the slants later.'

I turn and look behind me at the man who brought me to the speech. He looks a little confused. I don't blame him. I'm a little confused myself. But he waves his hand as if prodding me on to say more, so I do.

"Black people accuse us of having enslaved them. Now, it is true that we did, but they aren't slaves anymore, so they should just get over it. Some of them are still mad about it, but I like to think of it this way. If you bought a donkey and it didn't do the work you wanted it to, you would smack that donkey until it began to work. Same goes with a man. If the man doesn't work, you have to smack them around a bit. That's how property works. My television doesn't work sometimes. I smack it and get better reception. Should we treat people as property? No. People deserve equal dignity and respe….Wait, I mean, yes, we should. Black people are bad. Bad, black people, bad.

I look back again. The guy is giving me the thumbs up all the way.

"Anyway, black people are really, really bad. They don't respect law and order. They don't like cops. They don't like mayonnaise. If you don't like mayo then something must be wrong with you. I spread that shit all over everything. Maybe it's because mayonnaise is white. Have you ever thought of that? The black man is racist against mayonnaise. This shall not stand."

"Moreover, we can't trust people who mix our preciously pure white blood with all that black gooiness. White people should adopt white children. Black children will make their family all black and stuff. White women and men belong together. If you have a black girlfriend, like I do, then you're messing up our precious heritage. Did I say that I have a black girlfriend? That was a lie. Black women are all gross. She isn't my girlfriend. I have sex with her, but only because I feel sorry for her that she is black. It's like pity sex. We can all understand that."

"In conclusion, black people are bad. We should have them all exported so that they aren't here anymore to ruin our fun. They claim that America was built by the sweat and blood of their backs. That by their work alone they have elevated the white man and they only want the same consideration. We've climbed on their backs to reach the pinnacle, and now they're asking for a hand to reach that pinnacle themselves. Well, that's racist. They need to reach their potential through other people's hard work, the way we did. Maybe they should get their own slaves. They should have thought of that before they had Reagan pass the Emancipation proclamation. Sure, they were freed, but then they couldn't get their own slaves and now their bitching about it. Is that our fault? Assuredly not."

"I would like to thank you all for listening to me tonight. It is my hope that through non-violence that we can come to an equitable solution to our racial problems."

I stop, but there is no applause.

"Non-violence with a lot of guns! Get those darkies out of here! Go back to Australia where you belong, darky McDarkinson! We will peacefully fuck your shit up proper! White power forever!"

The crowd erupts with cheers. A chorus of Dixieland picks up in the back and reverberates throughout the crowd. The trailer park people in the back are hugging. The suits in the front are smiling. For a moment I feel like a god. Maybe being white isn't so bad after all. The wave of utopia spills out of me after a moment and I feel nothing at all. The crowd begins to disperse with good cheer. My hands clench on the podium. I wish the audience would start fighting so I could throw myself off the stage and into the welcome chaos. Nobody makes move one. What the fuck is wrong with these people?

"Aren't we going to go out and attack black people?"

"No. We're pretty much happy with the status quo. I'm going to go home and have a good soak in the tub."

See what I mean about white people? Shit.

I'm barely out to my car and that black chick is telling me that I'm on to speak to the blacks. Shit. Being a public speaker has me running my ass off. I start the car and head on over to the next gig.

"I PRESENT YOU WITH THE MAN WHO HAS TAKEN THE FOREFRONT OF THE BATTLE FOR OUR RACE. He stands, and we stand with him, united. Together we will restore liberty and equality and eliminate our race from decimation by whites."

I take the podium knowing that I am safe behind my disguise, but unsure enough to feel like this is a bad idea. I don't know why that black chick set me up for this, but I'm pretty sure that it's because she's sorry she ate all my food. But it's my risk, so maybe that's not it. Maybe she's just using this job as a way to get herself more food and while I'm out she's going to eat all of it and not leave any for me.

Anyway, the audience is staring up at me, some of them are shouting encouragement. They are wearing their Sunday best, and I wonder, after speaking with the whites, if it's customary to dress up before whipping yourself into a racial frenzy. I look to the back, but don't get the trailer park vibe I got from the whites. The crowds are there, but they don't look like they've crawled out of a hole. I make a mental note that poor whites dress poor. Poor blacks dress okay. It might be important to remember later.

I'm in my full get-up, but I was furnished with a baggier shirt with a larger hoodie. Coupled with the bandana around my face, I'm pretty well unrecognizable.

"My fellow blacks, I could call you by many names, but I choose black because that's how we identify each other. We are for the same cause. Let's just say that even if I were white, we would still be on the same side. So if I turn out to be a white guy, it would be poor sport to tear me apart. It's not that I am white, it's just worth remembering. I could call you Africans, but you were not born in Africa. You were born in America, but I cannot call you Americans, because we are not treated equally by white people. We are blacks. Our skin is our legacy and curse. Let's say you go out and try to find a job. Oh, you're black. No job. Let's hire this nice white guy instead. That's racist. Never mind that he went to school for five years and got a college degree. That doesn't mean anything. That's just racist. White people are bad. Bad, I say, bad."

"Let's face it. The white people kicked our ass a long time ago, and it still pisses us off. White people enslaved us and we worked our asses off to make this country great. What have we gotten in return? Nothing! What reparations have we gotten? Have you gotten any reparations? Have you? How about you, sir? I haven't either. It's time we make our demands heard! First, we should get housing, food, education, and enrichment activities befitting human beings. These things should be provided by the government. We demand that businesses hire people of color. It's racist to have all white people working in one place, even if those white people are more qualified. Black people will not serve in any military exercise. Our government does not represent us, so we will not die in wars on foreign soil."

"We demand our government to exempt black people, even Mexican black people, from all state and federal taxes. Taxes are to be paid by white people at the full rate, and Asians with a minor reduction because they're Asians and can't work as hard because they're small. America is run by, and controlled by white people. White people should be the ones to pay for it!"

"Where's my free house? Where is my free food? What do I offer in return? Nothing! This is like it is, my brothers and sisters, we were slaves for a very long time. We worked seven days a week for whitey. No days off. No vacation. What this means is that we have a lot of vacation time and weekend time accrued. Slavery lasted generations and generations! That means that vacation should last for generations and generations! This is a time of rest for us. This will be a time of rest for our children. Our grandchildren? They'll have to get of their asses and go to work, but we'll deal with those little bastards later. Reparations now!"

The audience is cheering. I look behind me and am getting thumbs up all the way. White people and black people love the shit out of me. What can I say? I rule.

"Anyway, white people are bad. They think that hard work and a good education can get you ahead in life. Have they tried being black? How about for just one day? No, they haven't. So how can they judge us? White people can't possibly understand black people. They think they can, but they can't. Black people are completely different than white people. Our bodies are built differently. Our brains work differently. We are much better at sports. How can the white man think we have an equal chance? They are smarter, but we can run faster. Black quarterbacks are the Uncle Toms of today! Wait…I mean that white and black people are equal. Whitey just gives us a raw deal."

"In conclusion, the riots used to be about cops. Cops are always giving us shit. Cops are always murdering us. Yes, it's true that more white people are killed by cops than blacks, but that's just a fact. It's not like it's true. Even if that fact was true, which it is, it's also true. Get what I mean? I don't know if I do either. Anyway, this isn't about cops anymore. It's about white people. White people have us down with industrialized racism and it needs to stop. We are only asking for what white people already have. They owe us because of slavery. They owe us big.

"I would like to thank you all for listening to me tonight. It is my hope that through non-violence that we can come to an equitable solution to our racial problems."

I stop, but there is no applause.

"Non-violence with a lot of guns! Get those whities out of here! Go back to Australia where you belong, whitey McWhiterson! We will peacefully fuck your shit up proper! Black power forever!"

The audience cheers. A chorus of 'Swing Low, Sweet Chariot' picks up from somewhere, but someone else has started singing, 'We Shall Overcome' and it gets all jumbled up and shit. I start singing Swing Low, because I love that fucking song. I can rock the shit out of it. I screw up the verses a bit, but I keep my voice low in case someone overhears me and figure out that I'm white. That would be a dead fucking giveaway.

I turn around and start to leave when the guy that brought me stops me by putting a hand right on my fucking chest.

"The time for revolution is now. Look at how all the brothers and sisters are with you."

"I'm not into revolution. Too much responsibility. I just like to fuck shit up."

"We need you. You will lead us to power over white suppression. Tonight!"

I try and get by him, but I'm fucking basically bum-rushed by four other blacks and taken through the crowd and out the front door of the auditorium to a really fucking nice looking Humvee. At least all of our asses fit into the car without getting squished. Good thing too, because these blacks are pulling our guns and popping clips into them. They are so fucking careless with the damn things that I'm sure one of us is going to get shot.

"Take one of these."

A fucking gun gets tossed over the back seat to me. Fucking tossed. I catch it and it fires right through the floor. The car lurches to the side of the street and all these black guys are screaming at me. I don't know what they fucking expected. You don't just go throwing guns at people. Or maybe people do. I don't know. I've never held a fucking gun before in my life. I'm not an idiot. I know to point the thing and shoot. I just don't know how sensitive the trigger is. The guys finally stop yelling at me and we get back on the road. I lightly test the sensitivity of the trigger. The gun goes off, blasting the guy next to me in the side.

"He shot me!"

"I didn't mean to!" I shot him again. The fucking trigger on this gun is *very* sensitive. I'm going to have to be more careful. I try and hand the gun over to the guy I just shot. I don't think I should be in charge of such a sensitive piece of equipment. I shoot the guy again. All of this happens in seconds, although it feels like longer to me. The car lurches off to the side of the road again. Guns are trained on me. I have my hands on the man I just shot to try and stop the bleeding. The guy in the passenger seat gets ready to shoot me in the face, but the driver pushes his hand away right when he pulls the trigger. The bullet ricochets off the heavy glass and hit the driver in the face. I pick up a gun from the guy I just shot and I shoot the guy who tried to shoot me.

Then, for good measure, I shoot the guy next to me again. He's really, really fat, and I'm mesmerized with the bullets going into that fleshy pudding body of his. I wonder where they stop inside of him. I shoot him again. It's like throwing pebbles into a mound of Jell-O, but I can't see inside. It doesn't matter much anyway. The dude died. This is so shitty, but I can't help myself from shooting him. It's a very tactile experience and I am a sensory orientated dude.

The car screeches to a halt and I kick open the door and start running. I hear screams. Shots are fired, but I don't feel any bullets whiz past. I just run. Soon I am lost in the concrete jungle.

I MADE IT ALL THE WAY TO FUCKING GRAND AVE. There weren't many people on the streets. Usually this place was popping, but not tonight. At least not right now anyway. The bars were pretty full up, but nobody was hanging on the street. There were people around the businesses cleaning up from the ongoing riots. I step in a mound of broken glass and kick the shards across the sidewalk.

"That's my window."

I look up to see a woman sweeping the glass toward the pile I just kicked. I feel a little shitty about messing up her work, but really I'm more worried about her giving me shit about it. The whole street is a fucking mess, it's not like I expected to mess up someone's mess. Or something like that.

"Sorry."

"No worries. I don't even know why I'm cleaning this up anyway."

I'm feeling pretty pleased that she won't give me any shit. She looks damn downhearted anyway. I take a look at her business. She's a fucking artist or something. I see fucked up paintings, fucked up as in destroyed, not the subject matter. There's bits of crafts lying around. Some still smoldering from last night's fires. The front store windows are toast. Even though her store is a fucking mess, I feel like it could have been a lot worse for her. Crafters make shit that nobody needs, let alone wants, so it's not like she had a lot of product looted. If this was a grocer or gun shop or something, everything would be gone. Art can be destroyed and still sell. All you have to do is combine the remnants of art and call it something else. Somebody somewhere will buy that shit. I've seen the shit they put in museums. Anything can be art if you can sell it.

"My insurance won't cover this."

"What?"

This bitch is still talking to me.

"The windows."

"Oh."

That's not my fucking problem. It's hers. This bitch probably has insurance, but just not the right fucking kind. This is why I don't own a business of my own. I fucking wash dishes. My fucking job sucks, but if the fucking restaurant goes up in flames, that's not a problem for me. I'll just go wash dishes somewhere else. This lady probably only has liability insurance or some shit. She's covered if someone slips on an oil painting or something. She's not covered if the populace rises up and destroys all her shit. Too fucking bad.

Am I a part of the problem? Do I have some stake in what happened to her? Sure I do. I'm just not held fiscally responsible for it. This bitch should have just stayed home and sold her shit on Etsy or something. It's not like artists make any fucking money. This place must have been a real pain in the ass for her. Hopefully, she'll find all this shit liberating. After all, she's not got much else. Who the fuck is going to buy this from her anyway. It's not like this area will ever really recover from the riots. I miss a day of work and I'm out sixty bucks. A day like this for her will cost her hundreds of thousands of dollars to rebuild. Do you think this artsy fartsy chick is going to cough up all that dough to rebuild here? Fuck no. Does she even have a choice in the matter? Fuck no. She's fucked.

"Five million dollars."

"What?"

Why the fuck am I still standing here? I should learn to fucking think and walk at the same time. I'm still standing in this pile of glass and now this chick is starting to talk to me again. Shit.

"Taxpayer money. That's what the tally is so far of what the riots are costing us. That's just in police and national guard costs alone."

"I don't live around here."

"You'll pay. We all will. The governor has been called to help. Ferguson is all of us. This is our identity. We will all pay."

"That fucking sucks."

She just fucking nods and keeps sweeping. I don't know where she plans on putting all the shit she's sweeping up. Maybe she'll use one of the burned out trash cans that are lying around everywhere. This shit doesn't need sweeping. It needs burying.

"I only have a couple of hundred in the bank. I think I'll go and get some groceries and shampoo and stuff so that I'm covered for the next couple of weeks. I don't know what else to do. I can't pay what I owe for this place. Why even pay the mortgage?"

I don't have an answer for that. I'm feeling super fucking uncomfortable, so I try and change the subject.

"Did you get out in the shit last night?"

"No. I was inside here. I thought that I could get them to leave me alone, but I ended up running into the back and just hiding behind my desk. I didn't even try to leave. Not even when they lit the place on fire. I was too afraid."

"That's kind of stupid – not running from a fire."

"I love this place. I guess I should say that I *loved* this place. I don't know how I'm going to dig my way out of this. I'm going to have to declare bankruptcy. I just know it. When it's all said and done, the insurance agencies around here are going to claim a loss in the billions of dollars. Sometimes I just don't get people."

I kick the glass again, not knowing what else to do.

"Good luck."

"I don't even know why I'm even sweeping this up. I don't know why I don't just put this broom down and walk away. It took years for me just to secure this place of my own. Now it's all gone."

I walk away from her. I look back over my shoulder and see her shaking her head and just looking at the ground. I wished her good luck, but I didn't really mean it. It's her fault that she put everything into a shitty store in a shitty neighborhood. Who the fuck around here was going to buy her shit. The riots probably saved her years of her life wasted on this enterprise. An arts and crafts store here is like trying to plant a garden in concrete – it just isn't going to fucking work.

WHEN I GOT BACK TO MY APARTMENT THE BLACK CHICK WAS STILL THERE. My place smelled really bad. It also had a lot more stuff than I remember having. There were plants and shit. Clothes everywhere. There were piles of girl stuff lying around, like makeup and shit. I don't know how I didn't realize it before, but I think that she moved in under my nose. We didn't talk about her moving in. I tried to think back about if I gave her a sign that moving her shit into my apartment was okay, but I don't think so. I've never had someone move in with me before, and I assume this shit is talked about.

"This place is a mess. I need to clean it up and you're going to help me."

"Is that any way to talk to me? It's not like you've done any cleaning since I've been here."

"I haven't made a mess."

"Maybe if you gave me some space I would be a little more organized with my things."

"This is my apartment."

"You see? I've been here for two weeks and you've still not shown me any respect. I've gotten you some good gigs for good money and you still treat me like shit."

The black chick starts laughing. I hate her fucking laugh. It's too loud.

"What's so funny?"

"I was just thinking that it's like reversed in this household. I'm like your pimp. Sending you out to get money, while I stay here."

"We're cleaning up."

"Fine, honey."

She gets up off her ponderous ass and starts putting her makeup into a large case. She's taking her damn time about it, and I don't see how she'll get done with that one simple task in under an hour. I go to the kitchen and start washing dishes, which I fucking hate. I wash dishes at my other job all day, so doing it at home really pisses me off. None of the dirty dishes are mine. I've been eating a lot of soup and I hate washing dishes so much that I just eat that shit out of the can cold. I tip that fucking can right back so I don't even have a fucking spoon to wash. She eats soup, heating it up in one bowl, and then putting it in another one to eat. Who the fuck does that? If she stirs the soup with one spoon, she uses a fresh one to eat it. Thank Christ she doesn't make food from fresh ingredients or else she would probably use every dish I have in the whole fucking place.

I wash and dry the dishes myself. Next I take a bottle of bleach spray and wash out the sink, counters, and the outside of the refrigerator. Thank Christ again that I never use my oven or any of that other shit. I would be cleaning the kitchen forever. I even dust afterwards. I fucking hate dusting. I mentioned before that my shit is never dusted. That's because I fucking hate it. My apartment is way too messy to ignore the chore and I do it. I think it's mostly because I don't want to go back into my living room and see that black chick still putting her makeup away. I don't even see why black people use makeup. They have black skin! That shit will never show up.

The kitchen is okay now and I go back into the room. The black chick did finish putting her makeup away and is now collecting her clothes and folding them up on the couch. It's a wonder to see my couch again, since all I've seen of it in the past couple weeks involves her ass lying down on it. I wonder if she has bedsores. I glance at the couch to see if she leaked any puss on it. I fucking hope not. It's the best couch I ever had. I picked it up last year after someone put it out for the garbage. Hauled that beast up the three flights myself. I'll be shit-swiggeld if I let some black chick weep bed sore pus all over it! Fuck! I have to get rid of this chick.

It's all my fault, I know. I should have spoken to her a long time ago. I should have asked her to leave, but I still feel shitty about it. I don't know how to talk to her. Black women are different. You don't have to say shit and they are all over you and your stuff. I still can't believe that she ate all that food I looted from that riot. I know I'm being all bent out of shape about something that happened so long ago, but that's the root of my problem. I can't talk to her, so all that old shit never got sorted out. Fucking women! Fucking black women! She'll probably hold all that money over my head too. It's true that if she wasn't here I would never had those speaking engagements and never gotten that gob of cash. Shit, that money pays for the running of my apartment for months. I do owe her that, but it doesn't mean that she gets to live here and put all her stuff her and everything.

"You're going to break a sweat working like that, honey."

"It's so fucking messy in here."

"We will get it cleaned up. Don't worry. Where do you want me to put my clothes? The bedroom?"

"I guess so."

What the fuck else was I going to say? I've heard that black women will scream your face off at the slightest infraction. I'm treading on dangerous ground here. I think about starting to help her clean up the rest of her stuff in the living room, but I don't really know where to start so I just go about dusting again. I even work on the windows a bit. I open a window in the back to let out some stuffiness, when I hear the black chick come back into the room. She's still cleaning up her stuff. Thank God. I take my time and wipe away some of the black grit on the window frame. There's not much to look at out the back window of my apartment. There's a little caged in parking area where you get to stash your car for an extra fifty bucks a month. A hell of a lot of good it does the people who can pony up that extra cash. That lot was awash with graffiti and debris. Some of the cars that were parked there looked as if they haven't moved for a long time.

"What are you looking at, honey?"

"There's nobody out there."

"Not usually during the day. Shitty parts of the world sleep in. Things only get rowdy at night."

She almost shoved me out of the way to take a look. Well, she didn't shove me, but she invaded my personal space which felt akin to a shove in my book. I backed off a step while she leaned forward and sighed, taking in a deep breath of the fresh air. I don't blame her since she's been smelling her own funk for days now.

"There is something we need to talk about.

"What?"

"I'm breaking up with you."

I shoved her out the window. She yelped a quick, small sound and landed head first onto the concrete parking lot. She didn't bounce. She landed almost completely vertical. Her lower half sagged into her upper half, rupturing her sides open in a quickly pooling pile of blood and organs.

It was an opportunity that I couldn't pass up.

I didn't really want to kill her. Just make her go away. I was able to break off our relationship without the awful conflict that usually goes with such things. My worry about her calling me a racist never came to fruition, thankfully. Unless she thought it on the way down. I will never know. You might think that I'm an asshole, a wimp, or a fraidy-cat or something, but you have to put yourself in my shoes. Many of you wouldn't be able to push someone out of a window. You can hate me all you want. I just really don't like conflict. I looked out the window, put everything was still quiet. I couldn't see or hear anyone. Good.

The first thing I did was go to the kitchen and grab some large black trash bags from under the sink. I don't take the fucking trash out too much because it's three fucking flights down and back up. I never think to take the trash out when I'm going out somewhere so it's always an extra trip. So I buy these big ass heavy duty lawn and leaf bags. It's arduous, but I don't have to go as often because I have those big fucking bags. I go the bedroom and jam all her clothes and makeup into one of the bags. She didn't have her stuff in my bedroom for long, but I hate that it was even there. That's my fucking space. In fact, the whole apartment is my fucking space and I want it fucking back.

Until I started packing up the black chick's shit I didn't realize just how fucking much of it she had. She infested every nook and cranny of my space. I found her shit all over the bathroom and living room. Only the kitchen didn't have any of her stuff in it, but I knew that already because I was just in there cleaning it. In the end I filled three of those fucking trash bags, so I was up and down the stairs three times before I got all of her shit dumped. Before I went up the last time I walked over to the bleeding mess which used to house her soul. Did I go through her pockets? You're sure as shit I did. What did I find? A fucking wad of cash. Almost a thousand bucks. She must have gotten a finder's fee for my speaking engagements or some shit. She was fucking holding out on me. I fed her and gave her a place to live, that money should have been mine from the start. She got me the gig, but I did all the fucking work. Shit.

I take the cash back up to my place and lie down on the couch. I'm tired as hell, so I fall asleep quickly. The sirens wake me up after a while when the cops come and are all over the place while they go over the body of the black chick. I'm pissed that they left their sirens on for so long because it's disturbing my sleep. I get up and close the window, go back to the couch and fall back asleep. I feel pretty fucking great when I wake up. It's night, for one thing, and I can't wait to get out and fuck shit up. The riots have been pretty hot and heavy and show no sign of calming down. The cops are still out there. Not as many of them, but a few, and they've got the whole back roped off and shit. I can see through my window that they've moved her body out of there. I take a deep breath and turn to my empty and fucking clean apartment and smile. It's good to have my place back again. I've learned a lot about living with someone and I need to take a little 'me' time. You know, get back in touch with myself, my wants, and my needs. Women just fuck everything up.

WELL, THE TIME IS NOW. I go to the bathroom to get all blackfaced up and ready to party. It's going to be a good one. The whites hate the blacks. The blacks hate the whites. Everyone hates the cops. Shit is going to go down. It's probably going to go down in a lot of places too. I can't wait! I have to decide where I'm going to go fuck shit up, because there should be a lot of places that burn tonight. The best part of what's going to happen is that the police and National Guard are going to be too spread out to really do shit to the rioters. Free reign is going to be a lot of fun. I like a little push back from the cops, but I don't want to be shut down and arrested before I can really get going. I need a small force of cops that's scared. Not too scared so that they start shooting. I just need them on their heels. That's my fucking cup of tea.

You know what? I think I'm going to go right back to Ferguson. That fucking place has always been a lot of fun. I'll bet most of the police are going to be near the St. Louis area protecting all the stuff that they think is important. Ferguson did burn a bit, but there is still a lot to fuck up. There's going to be a lot of angry people there and they're going to be fucking angry. I'll bet the whites are there too. Ferguson may be a shithole, but there's still a lot of fun to be had. We fucked up Grand Ave. the last time, but there are still a lot of places that could use a good raising. Tonight is going to be fucking balls, man. Fucking balls.

I go to the bathroom to put the shoe polish on my face, but realize that the fucking tin is empty, and I mean bone fucking dry. Looks so clean inside that I might have licked it out like a ten dollar whore. I could go with the light brown or even fucking grey, but I don't really see the point. When I put the bandana around my face and the hoodie hood down I look pretty well covered. I know I should probably go out and buy some more shoe polish to cover my face, but that will take too much time. I am so jazzed about getting out there that this will have to be good enough.

I set out and take my car, drive it out to a pretty close spot, then get out of the car and hoof it to the party. I brought a nice aluminum baseball bat and I can feel the blood pulsating in my tight-fisted grip on the handle. I smack cars as I walk down the sidewalk. Some alarms go off. Most of the cars here are too shitty to have good alarm systems so I just dent the fuck out of them. It's fucking great. It takes a pretty good swing to take out car windows, so I stick to denting the door panels or the hood. I have to stop myself and keep moving. If I stay too long smashing cars I will be picked up for sure. I think I see people starting to come out of their houses to see what all the noise is about. I stop beating cars and head toward the sounds of pissed off people and the sirens of cars.

Sweat is trickling off my face. I'm all warmed up and ready to go. I cross through to the crowd and find the rowdies. I swing my baseball bat into the car that they are already fucking up beyond recognition. They're black guys. Go figure. My bat does quick work on the side windows and the side mirror. Some black tries to take the bat away from me and I shove him back. He yells that he wants a swing, but I know if I give it up he won't ever give it back, so fuck him. He keep hollering at me, but I just smash the car and ignore him. I back off as a group of them starts rocking the car, finally tipping it over. The fucking car catches fire and I turn and run with the others before the impending explosion. A flash of fire and sound behind me. That fucker *went up.*

I move with the gang of blacks that has become my own. We wreak havoc with each small stop. I take out windows and smash parking meters. I fucking hate parking meters. Who carries change anymore? My crotch is already soggy from getting off, but I'm hardly done. I've just started this shit. Here they come. I knew they would. A group of whites. Fucking skin-heads, by the looks of them, come tromping down the street directly toward us. It's a better sight than the cops, let me tell you, but not exactly.

Cops can stop a riot before it starts. Fucking skin-heads are looking for one thing, blood. I take a look at my cronies and they look young, vibrant, and strong. But the fucking whites look older, harder, like they've been bashing black faces in for a long time. I drop back in line until I am behind my black brothers, take off my bandana and rip my hood back. When the front line of the blacks crash into the whites, I swing from the back and cave in the head of a young man who looked more scared than angry. The whites make quick work of the blacks.

Now that they're close I can see the Nazi tattoos. Fucking Skin-heads. They don't fuck with me any. Some of them shove me. I'm white, but not a fucking skin-head, so they don't want me to take any of their fun. At the end of the melee, four blacks are down, including the one I smashed in the back of the head. The whites keep moving forward and now I find myself a part of their group. We're hunting blacks.

I have to keep telling myself that we're hunting blacks because all I want to do is keep mashing shit up with my baseball bat. The skinheads aren't down with that at all. They're just wanting to fuck people up. Not just black people either. They're after white people who are standing with blacks. They're after the fucking peaceful protesters. I don't think this is a good time to bring up the fact that I've had a black girlfriend for the last couple of weeks. They wouldn't like that. They would probably like the fact that I pushed her out the window.

Anyway, hanging with the white guys is cool, but not totally my style. They've targeted their aggression, which actually hampers my ability to get off. I want mayhem. I *need* mayhem. I crave mayhem. These skinheads are just racist pricks. They're also kicking ass. It's not too surprising why. These guys are looking to kick ass while the other people don't have the same agenda. If you had a group of black toughs who were all jazzed up to fight, things would be a lot more interesting. All you get with this group is a bunch of rowdies bowling over anyone in their path. Beating up people who can't fight back isn't fucking fun. I don't get off on that shit. I like to fight people who can fight back. Fighting people who aren't ready to fight is like trying to sharpen a knife on Jell-O. It's not going to fucking work. Punch someone in the face who turns around and smashes you in the temple with an overhand right, that's fucking beautiful.

I leave the fucking skinheads as soon as possible. They have an agenda for something larger than themselves. My whole agenda involves me and I'm afraid my apathy might show through and I'll get beat up. Fuck that. I see some cops up ahead, so I take off my bandana and put my hood back. I don't expect them to bother me one fucking bit as I jog past them, but they do.

"Hey, you! Stop!"

I'm still carrying the fucking bat. Shit.

I put on speed and easily outrun them. All that fucking gear weighs them down too much, and they've got too much on their minds to go chasing after some crazy white guy with a bat. I'm thinking I'm in the clear when I get a sharp pain in my right shoulder. I drop the bat and put my hand over the wound. I've been fucking shot! I jizz my pants immediately. This is awesome! I've never been shot before. I start laughing, keeping up my run. I take my hand away from my shoulder, expecting to see a smear of glorious bullet wound blood. Fucking nothing. Fucking rubber bullets. If semen could go back up a dick, mine fucking would have. What a fucking buzz kill.

Then I fucking see it. Fire. Glorious fire. Half of a block has gone up in flames. I can feel the heat on my skin as I close in on the chaos. Firetrucks with screaming sirens get to the blaze. It makes me laugh. There are only fucking two of them. Useless against such an inferno.

Flaming debris litters the ground and I pick up the best of it. Holy fuck, it burns my hands, but I don't care. I punch in windows and toss the burning debris inside. My hands are ripped apart from the broken glass, but I don't care. Others band around me, smashing in the building's door and windows, tossing in flaming objects, trying to set the whole block afire. Sometimes the blacks punch and kick me. I fight those fuckers back until they think of something better to do. Most just ignore me.   People run out of the burning buildings at the same time that others run inside of them. People trying to save their lives or steal to make it through another week. I stop and admire the throng pushing in and out against each other. I jizz my pants again before I can get into the middle of them. I don't push, pull, or fight the flow of energy. I move back and forth with the crowd like a wave. I cum again. Beautiful.

A jet of water hits us all and we go tumbling to the concrete like wheat falling before a cutting scythe. The firefighters turned the fucking hoses on us. A blast hits me right between the shoulder blades, tearing the shirt off my back and bruising my flesh. I skid along the pavement and slam into a wall. I can't stop cumming. I know that if the firefighters are using their water for crowd control, they are neglecting the fires. Those fuckers must be burning out of control. I can't remember American's turning firehoses on other Americans since the LA riots. A blast of water hits me again. The air is torn out of my lungs. I am slammed against the brick building wall and cannot move. Just as I am about to pass out from pain and lack of air, the water jet is turned on others. This is fucking awesome. I'm here to tear shit up, even if it is myself.

I listen for them above the roar of the water. Where are you my lovelies? I've so wanted to make your acquaintance. There they are. Barking and howling, pulling against their cop master's chains, the dogs. I stand up, barely able to get my muscles to remember how to work. I see the dogs in a ragged line in front of what must be fifty cops. The firefighters have turned their hoses back at the burning block of homes and businesses. I lift my arms to the sky as the cops release the dogs upon us.

"Come to me, my lovelies."

I was hit by two huge German Shepherds. The first one kind of gave me a shot to my hip and went after the guy behind me. The second one took me while I was off balance, knocking me onto my back. I gave the dog my arm and it bit down hard. Holy fucking hell, that hurt. I jizzed my pants real good. This dog chose me for a reason. Fucking police dogs know the fuckers who want to get off and try and take them out of the equation fast. I knew that punching the dog wouldn't do shit but make it bite down harder, so fuck off with that idea. I know I have to act quickly or else I'm going to get a beat down by the cops that are coming hard on the dogs' heels.

Let me tell you something about fucking police dogs. They live off of fear. They love it when that have some poor asshole on the ground, screaming his head off, and trying to crawl away. They rip their skin, shred the poor bastard's clothing, and they fucking love it. Police dogs are touted through elementary schools and nursing homes as if they are the nicest things ever. That is bullshit. They are fucking assholes. Animals like to get off just like people do, and these fucking dogs love scaring the shit out of people.

For a moment I let my anger take me over. I'm going to fuck this dog up. I rear my arm back to punch the dog, but the shot barely has any power to it. The dog shakes me like a dead cat. I can feel my fucking guts bouncing around in my insides. I lay on the ground, totally fucking done. That dog that just kicked my ass is now sitting two feet away from me, panting and barking, looking very well pleased with himself. Here's a note to all of you: Police dogs will kick your ass. Don't bother fighting them. Holy shit.

The cop smacks me right in the back of my right thigh with his fucking nightstick. He doesn't even tell me to roll of my stomach or anything to cuff me. The shot fucking hurts, but even rolling over onto my side and groaning makes the fucking German Shepard growl. Now what the fuck am I going to do? There's a big fucking dog and a cup with a weapon. What the hell is my beat up ass going to do? The cop must think I'm going to do something because he's still kicking my ass. As if the shots from the people, the firehose, and the dog didn't do enough damage on their own. I think the cop's finally done and going to arrest me, then a fucking brilliant thing happens.

I'm trampled.

This is beautiful. I don't feel the boots of militarized cops. I feel sneakers, sandals, and even a fucking croc or two. I'm no longer being beaten. The fucking dog is yowling. I look up to see people beating it with sticks, bricks, and stabbing the fucking thing with knives. There's a cop crying his ass off while he's trying to get at his dog. Pussy. He wasn't crying while beating me up while I was helpless. Fucking crybaby prick. The people are fighting back. The cops are losing.

I feel like a badly used fucktoy, but I get my ass up to my feet. I limp along and catch a glimpse of myself in the spider-webbed, broken storefront glass. I'm moving like an old man on his last legs, but I'm smiling from ear to ear. The cops had the whites and the blacks snowed for a while; that this was about racial issues, but it's actually about cops being assholes. A little swarm of thug ass cops made white and black pick each other off the ground and turn on their true enemy – law and order.

Law and order is great and all, when someone is fucking your shit up and you need help, but most of the time it just gets in your way. Law keeps everything fair, and we the people love that as long as it's fair in our favor. When you cut it right down to the bone, everyone loves to take revenge on cops. Every single one of us has a story where a cop was being a total asshole for no reason. Even cops hate other cops, and I'm sure, at the midnight hour in their beds, cops lie awake at night hating themselves.

Of course I'm not talking about myself. I don't give a shit about cops, black people, or white people. I just don't give a fuck about anything really – except what I get to do now. Now that the fucking dog isn't kicking my ass anymore, I'm free to riot as I please, and I please very much thanks.

The cops aren't fucking with me anymore – they're dealing with the blacks and the whites.

The whites and the blacks aren't fucking with me anymore – they're dealing with the cops.

The Mexicans and Asians aren't fucking with anybody – because they really just don't fuck with anybody. Those guys are cool.

"Give me fire."

That's all I can think about. I want fire. I want the whole fucking world to burn. The fucking firefighters aren't anywhere around. The cops can't keep them safe anymore. I hear bullets flying, but I can't tell whether they're from the cops or the people. It's fucking martial law. I can do whatever I want. I find a building that's burning pretty well and go inside. I take a couple of things that are well lit and run them over to the next building. It's so fucking easy to spread a fire along this block of row house businesses.

Then the fucking bottom drops out.

"Freeze!"

Now who the fuck says, 'Freeze' anymore? I turn around and see this old dude pointing a fucking pump action shotgun at me. All I can do is stare down that huge ass looking barrel as this guy keeps yelling at me. I can't understand a word that he's saying. He's trembling and I'm not sure if he's just go the old man shakes, or is just scared out of his shit. I don't see how he can be scared since he's the one pointing the fucking shotgun. I have every right to be scared shitless. The gun looks brand spankin' new, like it's never been fired. This prick must have picked up the heater recently, trying to make himself feel safe in his own neighborhood with all this civil unrest shit going on. Fucking gun companies love the shit out of civil unrest. It boots sales through the fucking roof.

"You just stay right there. I'm going to call the cops."

"I'm not fucking moving. Just don't fucking shoot me."

He's now holding the shotgun on me with one hand and trying to dial up the cops on his cell with the other. He's so damn shaky that I'm sure the gun will go off and blow my stomach through my spine.

"It's busy."

The old guy is looking at me like it's my fault that 9-1-1 isn't working, but I don't know what the fuck he expected. The whole fucking city is probably trying to dial 9-1-1, and they are shit out of luck if they think the cops are going to show up. All the cops are pretty damn well busy right now dealing with the rioters. They don't give a fuck about this old guy or me.

"I'm placing you under citizen's arrest."

"You're going to do what now?"

"You are under arrest."

"Okay."

"Why are you doing this? Why are you destroying my city?"

Now I fucking get it.

This old guy has decided to make me the face of this whole fucking thing. He's been sitting in his shitty little rent controlled apartment, watching his whole world go to hell, and wanting to know why. Now that he's got one of those rioting fuckers (me) at gunpoint, I'm going to have to be the one to answer his questions.

"Look, it's not personal. I just like fucking shit up."

"Don't you have a conscience? Look what you've done. Don't you care?"

"No. I don't. Sorry."

"You're burning my home! You're burning my life! You have to stop!"

This guy was fucking crazy. I don't really ever feel the need to help my fellow man, but now was the time. This guy needed straightening out.

"Look, fucking shit up is awesome. I cum all the time. Burning shit is fucking fun."

He wasn't having it.

"You can't live your life through destruction. You are hurting so many people. Real people. Not to mention what this does to our city. It will take decades to recover from this– if we ever do. You can't just think about yourself. You have to think about your fellow man."

"But we're both white. Don't you think I'm awesome? Aren't we on the same side?"

"No. We are not on the same side. You are the enemy of everything I hold dear and true in this life. We have nothing in common."

I hit him with a brick.

The fucking old guy dropped his gun barrel enough so that I felt safe to smash him one. He was too busy talking to me about shit that didn't make sense and he forgot he had put me under citizen's arrest. Whatever the fuck *that* is. Maybe I should try citizen's arresting someone sometime. It sounds pretty fucked up. Maybe I can get a jizz out of it.

My brick caught the dude on the forehead, knocking him flat on his back. The shotgun went off, but I don't think he was even conscious to feel the recoil, seeing that his arm shot back all wonky and shit. I bet it dislocated. It's his own fucking fault. Nobody that old should be trying to shoot a gun like that. What the fuck was he even pointing it at me for? That's fucking dangerous.

I felt kind of shitty about hitting him with a brick. It didn't get me off at all. He wasn't pushing back at me or anything. It's kind of like trying to sharpen a knife with Jell-O, or whatever I said before. I really fucking like that phrase. I made it up myself. Quote me on that, bitch.

The guy started convulsing. I guess I smacked him in the brain or something, because he was really fucked up. He was making odd gurgling noises as he flopped around. I turned him on his side and pulled his tongue out from the back of his throat so he wouldn't choke and shit. Then the guy shit himself. It was a fucking mess and took my hard-on away completely. It made me think about a dog I had growing up who was all seizury and shit. That dog shit himself all the time too. My Dad shot it in the head with a .22 in the garage. He was all worried that someone would hear the shot and call the cops. My mom wanted to take the dog to the vet or the shelter to be put down, but my dad was having none of it. The fucking vet would have cost him an arm and a leg. The fucking shelter was a hundred bucks to put the dog down. A fucking .22 bullet costs pennies.

It was an easy choice. Seeing the old guy and thinking about the dog made me think of my parents. I wondered how they were doing. It had been years since I had seen them last. I felt all weird inside, so I put my hand in my pants and jacked off until I wasn't thinking about them anymore and got my hard-on back.

I picked up the brick and smashed the old guy in the face until his skull split open and his brains leaked out all over the floor. I hate killing people. It makes me feel kind of shitty, but fuck that guy. That guy was an asshole. My hard-on was starting to leave again and I had to do something to get my mojo working again.

I picked up the shotgun. Oh, Yes.

I just fucking shot that shit in every direction until I spent the fucking thing. Holy shit that felt good. It blew my fucking shoulder all to hell, but fuck that, I'm all beat up anyway. There's not a whole lot that can make me feel better than just firing off a fucking shotgun. I don't own a gun myself. I'm kind of scared of the fucking things. It's not that I'm afraid of someone shooting me. I'll probably shoot myself. If there's a gun around I'm going to fucking shoot it. I just can't help myself. If I go to a friend's house and see a gun, I'm going to fucking shoot it. I won't shoot it at anyone, but holy fuck I'm going to shoot that thing. It doesn't make me cum, though, so guns are pretty fucking useless in that regard. They just get my shit going again. I fucking love this shotgun. My hard on was back. I felt great. I felt alive! Holy shit, I had to get the fuck out of that building. It was almost totally engulfed by flames.

I dropped the shotgun and ran out, slapping the fire out that was burgeoning on my right pants leg. I started coughing and hacked up a pretty disgusting wad of brown phlegm onto the street. There were a few people milling about, watching the fire, but no one paid me any attention. All that smoke made me thirsty as a motherfucker. I walked down a couple of blocks to a corner store. It was all broken in and pretty well looted, but there's always shit lying around on the ground. I found a 20 ounce bottle of root beer. I fucking hate root beer, but what the fuck are you going to do? I had to wash out my fucking throat.

The root beer went down okay. I tried to find something else, but there wasn't anything else to drink. There were still some cans of food and shit, but I had no interest in those right now. Right now I wanted to do something particularly rioty. I know that's not a word, but shut the fuck up. It works. I ran out in the middle of the street, grabbing people, and pulling them as close together as I could. I stood up on the hood of a burned out 90s Chevy Caprice.

"Hey, you people! This is our chance to really make a difference! Some of you hate white people. Some of you hate blacks. Some of you are just trying to get off! We can all sort out our own shit in our own way together! This whole shit mess didn't start out as a black and white thing. It started out as a cop thing. We can all come together with our hatred of cops and cop violence. We can strike back together. Who's with me?"

I was hit with a brick in the knee. I didn't realize that all the people I gathered together were black. People started putting the boots to me when I heard a couple of gunshots and people screaming. The blacks ran back and cop feet started walking over and around me. Just like I was saved from the rioting blacks by the cops, I'm now saved by the cops from the rioting blacks. Somewhere in the back of my mind I'm wondering where the fuck all the white people are.

I already know the answer. The people in charge are fine with the status quo. White people don't give a fuck. What I expected to be a huge climax of rioting triumph turned out to be anticlimactic bullshit. I was picked up off the ground by a couple of cops, sat down on a fucking curb, and given a Red Cross blanket. There was nothing I could fucking do. I sat there, saved by the cops. Fuck my fucking life.

I'LL BET YOU'RE JUST SITTING ON YOUR ASS READING THIS SHIT AND JUDGING THE FUCK OUT OF ME. I don't give a shit. I just want to get off. You just want to get off. Everybody just wants to get off. That's all that life is about really. Some people get off with drugs, others with sex, others with money, achievement, Zen, accumulation, ejaculation, power, infringement, you fucking well name it, and someone is getting off on it. Five year old Little Debbie Snack Cakes? Somebody, somewhere out on this wide green earth is getting off on those. How? I don't really care to know.

I get off on rioting. I love that shit, and fuck you if you think that I need a real reason to do it. It's not a fucking jump of consciousness to realize that a lot of people love to fucking riot and a lot of them love it for the same reason I do, which is no real reason at all except they like to let loose and fuck shit up. I think that if you give ten people ten bricks, tell them they won't get into trouble, and say they can throw it through a storefront window, eight or nine of those people are going to do it. I'm not saying it's wrong or whatever, I'm just saying that people find breaking windows satisfying. Especially if they know it's something they're not supposed to do.

What about those one or two people who didn't throw the brick through the glass? I wouldn't hesitate to say that there must be something wrong with them. Let's say there's two of those no-window-breaking-fucks. The first one is probably mentally handicapped. He's got a sensitivity to noise or some shit like that, so he knows he's going to fuck himself over if he takes out the window. So he doesn't do it. The handicapped, like everyone else, want to get off. Breaking windows fucks up this guy's vibe. He doesn't do it. The other person? He doesn't do it because he thinks it's wrong. He's morally against doing such a dastardly thing as breaking a window. You know what? He's not wrong. Breaking shit for the sake of breaking shit is wrong. It's fucking awesome, but wrong. This last dude is the very small section of the population who still does the right fucking thing when the lights are out and no one is watching. He sets his moral compass and that fucker doesn't budge.

Good for that fucking guy. He's going to die with the biggest, most painful set of blue balls ever, but good for that guy. Way to do the right thing, fucker. That guy probably gets off by being high and mighty. A virtue is its own reward type of shit. So maybe he doesn't have blue balls after all. He's just getting off like the rest of us. And he doesn't even have to break a fucking window to do it. I wish I was like that. Breaking windows can be a lot of work. Once I bounced a brick off a bullet proof glass window. It came right back at me and smacked me in the gob. That fucking hurt.

There's not really much to say about the whole cops and blacks thing. Cops have been fucking with people for as long as there have been cops. Blacks break a lot of crimes, probably more than whites by my reckoning, but maybe not. Maybe they're just really shitty at crime so they get caught all the time. Anyway, cops bug the shit out of black people – even the ones who aren't committing any crimes at the time. That's a fucking fact and it's pissing the black people off. The only way to make this better is for blacks to stop committing crime, which won't happen.

The other way the situation could get better is if the cops stop predominantly harassing blacks, which won't happen either. No matter what you do, shit is going to remain the same. White people and black people will never fucking get along. Ever. I fucking know that some of them get along just fine, but it can't be real. White people and black people are just different. It's as plan as…well…black and white. Some of you might disagree with me, but you're fucking wrong. People of the same color can hardly get along. Now you think that people who look so fucking different than each other can interact peacefully. Ludicrous. If you have two groups of people fighting they are going to all go on the side that looks like them and try to fuck up the others. That's just how it fucking is. Deal with it. It doesn't mean that you have to go out of your way and fuck up someone of a different color. That's racist. I just say that we should stop trying to understand each other.

White people are still shit at rioting. Another fact for you, darlings.

I don't know what to really fucking tell you about this shit anymore. I'm sitting on this pile of rocks and my ass is burning a little bit. I think it's the fire that's heating up all the debris I'm sitting on. I hope is not a venereal disease. I'm a little fucking beat up, and a little fucking delirious. In fact, I've never felt so good in my life. I think I got this whole rioting thing out of my system. I mean, look at this place. It's burned to the fucking ground. Where can I go from here? I am at the pinnacle of self-actualization. I needed some juice, found it right here at home, and squeezed that motherfucker for all it was worth. Sure, this place is all fucked up now and I probably don't have a job anymore, but I really don't give a fuck at the moment. I got mine. And, when I think about it, everyone else got theirs too. Maybe. People got to hate on other people. We all got to tear shit up. The problem with other people is that they don't get a sense of fulfillment from it, like they're fucking their asses off and never get to jizz. Well that's their fucking problem. I jizzed so fucking much that my balls are probably turned inside out.

I'm probably done with all this shit, but I don't know. Fat people are always saying they should diet right after they eat three pizzas, and they are sure as shit serious about it then, but being serious about dieting with a full stomach is one thing. Sticking to it when you're hungry as shit and your stomach acids are slowly eating away at your fat stores is another. I'm savaged, but maybe the hunger will return. Only time will tell.

I just realized that I never told you fucks my name. You can call me Stu, or Bill, or James, or George, or anyone, for that matter. I really don't give a fuck. It doesn't even really matter when you think of it. I'm just a shitty guy, with a shitty job, who likes to get off. And I will get off any way I can. Fuck me and fuck you. I'm out.

THAT'S WHEN THE FUCKING BALTIMORE RIOTS HIT.

I couldn't even tell you where Baltimore is on the map. I found out that it's in a shitty little state called Maryland. It's one of those small fuckers on the Eastern side of the map. You've probably never even heard of it. It's not fucking New York or anything. Maybe I'm in the minority, and everyone knows about Baltimore. What the fuck can I say?

It's been quiet as fuck around here for a long time. At least it feels long to me. To everything there is an ebb and a flow. Riots are the same way. No matter how pissed off people are about something, they just run out of steam after a while. For a couple of weeks Ferguson was all the world was talking about, now they're all talking about Baltimore. Nobody gives a shit about Ferguson anymore. Nobody gave a shit about Ferguson before the riots and now it's been relegated back to anonymity. It's nothing more than a Wikipedia page.

Baltimore is way the fuck away from me. I've traveled a long way to riot, but it kind of pisses me off. I got used to having all this shit in my backyard, and now if I want to get off I have to drive like twenty fucking hours. That's a lot of fucking gas money and I don't fucking carpool.

There's been a lot on the news and on YouTube and shit about cops messing people up. I saw one of this one black guy who was gunned down by a cop. This other dude was filming with his camera phone over a fence. The filming guy sounded so fucking freaked out by what he saw, and I don't fucking blame him. What if the cop saw him filming? That cop would have shot that guy too. There was another one in California where a bunch of Sheriffs beat the shit out of a white guy. There were like ten Sheriffs and they all took a shot at the dude while he lay defenseless on the ground. I'm not a Sheriff. I don't know what their training manual says or anything, but I don't think that it tells you to make sure you punch or kick a guy who's on the ground with five other Sheriffs already laying on him. That fucking guy is lucky that he wasn't killed.

These cops are the fucking stupid ones. There are cameras everywhere. Nothing that you do is off camera anymore. What did they think would happen? They think that they can do whatever they want and nothing will come of it. The population says differently. The people are fighting back.

I guess what I'm trying to say is that the whole black and white thing has taken a backseat to civilians versus cops again. Everything is a fucking pendulum. Just like I fucking told you.

I've fallen back in anonymity too. Nobody gives a fuck about me anymore. That's just how I like it. I don't really like other people very much, and I've had my fucking fill of interactions over the last few weeks. I'm suffering a major case of blue-balls too. After all that riot cumming my internal sperm bank must have been working overtime. My balls are fucking huge, but there's no getting off for me. Every time I piss I think of all the wasted sperm that's coming out with my urine. I think I heard about that in Health Class or something when I was in high school. Anyway, I have a real need to get off. I think I'll have to drive all the way to Baltimore to do it.

Shit.

Work has pretty much gone on the same. The boss had to hire two new guys, as the black guys that tried to rape me never came back to work. You'll remember that there were three black guys that tried to rape me that night. The third one is still there. We kind of looked at each other the first shift we were back together, but we didn't say anything. I guess we're just both pretending that what happened never actually happened. That's all fucking right by me. Fuck that guy. If he tries it again he knows he's going to get his dick sliced off with my taint razor. I keep that fucker taped to me at all times. I've added another line of defense to my ass as well, because the last time was too fucking close for comfort. I shit myself, then the taint razor, and as a final defense I have the sandpaper. I superglued a couple of strips of sandpaper to the insides of my asshole about two inches in. If someone puts a dick up my ass they're going to lose the epidermis on their shaft on the first pump.

That's what I'm fucking talking about.

I don't have another girlfriend either. That black chick that I sent out the window was the last one. It's all about me again. That's just how I fucking like it. The cops never put her murder on me either. At least that's what I think. Nobody ever came around to talk to me about it. I guess one dead black chick doesn't amount to much.

I've walked the streets of Ferguson a couple of times for riot nostalgia's sake. The place is as fucked up now as it was. I don't think that the insurance companies are really chomping at the bit to pay up and rebuild. It doesn't look like a lot of the businesses will ever be coming back. It doesn't surprise me, but there's just not much left there now. I guess it sucks for the people that live there, but they can fucking move if they don't like it. It's not my problem.

I've got a little money stashed away from my speaking engagements that I plan on heading out to Baltimore with right after I get off of work. I've got something else too. I've got cop riot gear. It wasn't too hard to get ahold of. Cops were too spread out when the shit really hit the fan. I stripped one of their helmet and vest. I think I can finish off the outfit with a little bit of shopping. This shit is going to be awesome. I'm going to go cop. Rioting with a gun and a nightstick will be something a little different. I'll bet I cum buckets.

I almost sing while scrubbing the fucking dishes. I can't fucking wait to hit the coast.

TWO DAYS LATER I'M ROLLING INTO BALTIMORE. Let me tell you something. Baltimore is fucking nice. It's a whole lot cleaner than where I live. It's hard to believe that anyone has enough issues here to riot, but I guess a cop murdering someone in broad daylight is enough to light any fuse. I don't want to make Baltimore sound like some sort of utopia. It's not. By a long shot. But it's a damn far sight nicer than Saint Louis.

I didn't know anyone in Baltimore. I didn't have to worry about people recognizing me from over the internet, because here I'm going to go cop. I'm kind of pissed off that I couldn't get a riot shield, but I think I'll go over okay. The cops have been called from everywhere to be here. A white guy in a cop helmet and riot armor that doesn't fit the local mold won't be noticed too much. I just have to keep myself from humping parking meters.

I stop at this really shitty looking motel that hasn't seen a makeover in probably about thirty years. All I want to do is sleep through the day, so I don't need much. I just wanted cheap and I fucking got it. Thirty bucks a night isn't bad at all. The manager told me to keep my door locked and don't let anyone I don't know into the room. Fat fucking chance of that. The other people I see around here look like junkies or hookers or both.

I put my shit in the room and check the sheets. To my surprise, they look to have been cleaned recently. I strip the bed anyway and flip the mattress to the cleanest side and remake the bed. The room smells of cigarette smoke and mold. It has a small fridge, but it doesn't work. The television works and I put on the news. I don't know shit about Baltimore and I'm hoping the news can give me a clue as to where the shit it going down.

I take out the Wal–Mart bags from when I shopped for cop clothes and lay everything out. I just chose black. Black pants, black button down shirt, black sunglasses, and black shoes. Everything looks pretty well ready to go. I put the armor and helmet down next to it. It will be nice not to have to rub all that shoe polish shit on my face.

The news isn't telling me shit. I get up and take a shower and lie down on the bed naked. The office manager tells me to fuck off when I ask for a wake up alarm at midnight. I set the alarm clock next to my bed and go to sleep, lying on top of my fake cop clothes.

MY ALARM CLOCK RINGS. It's probably been going for a very long time because there's banging on both common walls of my room. I've probably been awakened by the wall banging and not the alarm. Thank God for shitty motel rooms and their paper thin walls. I could have slept through the whole night and missed the fun.

I put on my cop clothes and look in the mirror. I look like a fucking douche. Perfect – just like a cop. I make my face into a snarl and settle it down to a hard lined stare. I try and mimic the detached cop look and I think I can pull it off. It will be hard as fuck to keep myself from smiling during the riot, but hopefully everyone else will have other things on their mind by then and not notice my dumbass smirk. I take out a knife and put it in my shoe. I strap on my police baton and put a revolver at my hip. I wish I had a fucking shield.

I step out of my motel room and go to my car. The motel is fucking alive with people. This fucking sucks. I should have thought of that before I picked such a shitty motel. Some of the people go back inside their rooms as I walk out of mine. Some just look at me with disinterest. When you're in the city, people who are only kind of bad know you have much better things to do than hassle them. As long as you are just a mildly bad person, you can get along fine in any city.

I take the highway and follow the signs towards the baseball stadium. There's sure to be a lot of people there. Turning off the exit ramp, I can already see them. There's a teeming horde of people in a line walking toward the cops. They are linking arms in the front. Men and women behind them are holding up their hands like they're surrendering. What the hell is that all about? If you don't want the cops to shoot you, putting your fucking hands in the air is a fucking stupid way to go about it. Maybe it's a black thing. How the fuck should I know? I'm just a dumbass white dude.

The whole protest was a fucking joke anyway. All they did was yell a bit. Nobody threw a brick. Nobody shot tear gas or anything. It was boring as fuck. I left pretty dejected. I felt really bad for myself.

I DIDN'T REALLY LIKE BEING A COP. It's a whole lot more responsibility with half the jizzing. There was something about it though. When you serve and protect you just start wanting to serve and protect the shit out of everybody. I needed to restore order! I started with my motel. It was pretty quiet, but quiet crime is sometimes the most devilish of all. These people didn't need to know that I wasn't a cop. I wasn't out to hurt anybody like some vigilante prick. I am here for peace and I am going to peace the fuck out of these people.

The people who were staying in the room to my left were the first ones I needed to check out. They were the least quiet of the quiets. I could hear a little moaning and bed thumping. There was some fucking going on and I had to make sure that everything was on the up and up. If there's one thing I've learned that I can't stand in all my hours as a fake cop, it's nefarious fucking.

I knocked on the door with my nightstick. I kept the helmet and vest on and all that shit. It was hot and weighty, but I had to protect myself. Safety first. A man inside told me to fuck off. Telling a cop to fuck off is a felony, at least to my understanding of the law. I kicked open the door and fell on my face in the room. That door was a lot shittier than I thought. The thing splintered like kicking through cardboard. I looked up. A lamp shattered over my helmet. I swung out with my nightstick and cracked a boney knee. A woman shrieked and I swung again, making sure I broke her shit good. You can't be too careful when breaking a woman's knee. Women's knees are a tricky thing.

I stood up and saw a naked man on the bed. He was fucking a chubby chick and not paying me much attention. The woman I hit was writhing on the floor. She wasn't screaming, but she was moaning pretty loudly. She had a large red weal along her forehead. I looked down at my nightstick and grimaced. Was this fucking stick hitting bitches when I wasn't paying attention? I will have to keep my eye on this damn thing. A weapon is dangerous when it develops a mind of its own.

"Police Force Mega Zero! You are all under arrest for consensual fucking."

"I told you to fuck off!"

I jabbed my nightstick in the man's ass. He arched his back. The chick under him moaned. The man turned his face to my and smiled.

"Okay. You can stay."

Holy shit, this guy was fucking crazy. I jammed my nightstick further up his ass to show him that I meant business. His moan turned into a yelp as the stick jammed into his ass up to the hilt. I put my foot on his back and shoved. My nightstick came out of his ass with an audible pop. I'm going to need to bleach this damn thing. The girl underneath the guy screamed. She reached down and pushed the guy off her. He rolled off the bed and held his hands to his groin.

"You broke my dick!"

"His broken dick ripped my vagina!"

"Nobody is breaking anyone's dick under the eyes of the law!" Holy shit I love this police stuff. I have been living a lie with rioting. Policing is the best fucking thing on the planet. You can do absolutely fucking anything. I love the fucking law. "This man has ripped your vagina! He will be prosecuted to the fullest extent of the law!"

I stepped around the bed and knocked that vagina ripping asshole out with several smacks with the nightstick. I heard a little crack and hoped that I wasn't going to break my damn weapon. What will my Captain say? The chubby chick on the bed rolled onto her stomach and tried reaching for the phone.

"There are no phones in the eyes of the law!"

Another couple of smacks with the nightstick took care of the phone and the chick. Justice served. I looked around the room, didn't find any drugs or other nefarious paraphernalia. I walked back over to the chick with the broken knee and the head weal and put my foot on her chest.

"What is going on here? What's the story?"

"It's nothing." She was crying. I fucking hate it when chicks cry. "It's just a swinger's thing. We hooked it up on Craigslist."

"Really? They do that?"

"Yeah."

"Well…I guess you may all carry on! There are no crimes being committed here! You may go in peace. Selah."

I took my foot off her chest and walked out the door, making sure to close the broken thing as best as I could. These law abiding people needed privacy for their Craigslist fucking. There were a couple of people watching me leave. They were peeking out of their doors to see what the noise was about. They were probably breaking the law. A policeman's job is never done.

"Put your hands on your ankles and prepare to be searched!"

Their doors closed. There must be some dangerous deeds being done behind those doors. This was going to be a long fucking night.

THE SECOND MOTEL ROOM DOOR WAS IN MUCH BETTER SHAPE THAN THE FIRST. I was kicking it when a hole blew through the door and something knocked me onto my back. My stomach hurt like a bitch. I looked up and saw a smoking hole in my vest. That fucker shot me! He had better have a permit for that gun, or else it would be his ass. Luckily for him, he was in safe hands, for I had a gun too.

I put the barrel through the hole in the door and emptied the barrel. He screamed for me to stop shooting and that he had put his gun on the floor. I kicked the door again and this time it broke off at the bolt. I ran inside the room and the man shot me again. Again, he hit me in the chest. It hurt like a motherfucker, but that was okay. My headlong run wasn't stopped by the bullet and I tackled that man right across the hips. Just like football in fucking high school. I've still got it, baby!

The tackle sent us both into the wall behind him. His back made a sizeable dent in the rough plaster wall. He grunted and began to punch me. I tried to bite him, but it didn't do me much good. Fucking police helmets need a fucking hole in them so you can bite a motherfucker. These officers on the force must have been cops so long that they miss the obvious. I will have to write a strongly worded suggestion letter to the force. My life is at risk here! Being a cop is hell.

The man's knuckles buckled and crunched as he beat me on the head. I leaned back and head-butted the criminal prick right in the fucking mouth. His teeth rained down the front of his shirt and were quickly washed away with a torrent of blood that drained from his gums.

"Shooting a cop is a federal offense! Punching a cop is a federal offense! Bleeding on a cop is a misdemeanor or a fine of something. Whatever it is, you will be punished to the fullest extent of the law!"

The man began to sob as he held his hands to his chest. They were mangled from striking me in the helmet. Criminals are dumbasses. I sentenced the man to death in my mind. His crimes against cops were too much to just allow the man to live in functional society. I lowered my revolver and fired. The hammer hit, but no fucking bullets came out. Fucking gun was empty. There was only one thing to do.

I had to hang the prick.

I took the motel room iron and jammed it into the upper corner of the closet wall above the clothing rack. I helped the man to his feet and wrapped the cord around his neck. I thought about reading him his rights, but I had already sentenced him to death so I thought I could just skip it and be okay. I like to do things by the fucking book. Being a cop is awesome!

I ran into a problem when I tied the man's neck up. He was choking really well, but he wasn't dying. The fucker was still getting air and it was my fault. His fucking feet were still planted on the ground. Little gasps of air were getting into his lungs where there should be none. This was fucking up my justice.

I thought about tearing up the floor beneath his feet, but that would take too long. Justice waits for no man. There was only one thing to do.

I had to cut off his legs.

The only cutting utensil at the ready was a Spork that I found on the counter in a Chinese food takeout tray. It didn't do me much fucking good. I stabbed that prick about ten times, didn't do much damage, and the fucking thing broke on me. Fuck. I used my quick thinking cop reflexes, or whatever, took my helmet off, and began chewing on his leg. It was only a couple of bites in that I had to grab a washcloth from the bathroom to stifle his screams. I got all the way to the bone in one leg and couldn't gnaw through that fucker. I was trying to think of something else I could do to get his legs cut off, but I was interrupted.

"Freeze! Police! Put your hands behind your head and step backwards slowly. Do not turn around!"

I DID AS THE MAN SAID. My blood drenched hands matted my hair as I entwined them. I stepped back slowly. I didn't want this person to shoot me. I didn't really know if he had a gun, but I couldn't turn around to fucking look. I'm not stupid. If I did that and he had a gun, he would shoot me for sure. I just had to assume. I used my top-notch cop assuming senses. I sensed this guy meant business. I sensed that he had a gun. I sensed that he wasn't a cop at all. He was trying to trick me.

After all, I am totally dressed like a cop. Any real cop that came into the room would use their own top-notch police senses and realize that I was just a cop doing some honest police work. I had the vest after all. I wasn't wearing my helmet, but it was right there on the floor for him to see. What the fuck was wrong with this guy? I knew what was wrong with him. He wasn't a cop.

He was probably this guy's accomplice. If that was the case, than this guy was sentenced to death as well for being an accessory after the fact. What facts, you might ask? All of them. This is real cop shit.

"Get down on your knees. Keep your hands on your head!"

"Are you going to shoot me?"

"I have a gun on you and I will shoot you if you make any sudden movements. You have the right to remain silent…"

The fake cop went on and on. I was really tempted to take a look over my shoulder and see what this guy was wearing. He could be giving me the fake cop routine while wearing a clown suit for all I knew. I'm not going down like that. No fucking fake cop in a clown suit is going to gun me down. No way. Good for me that I had a plan. I saw this Sylvester Stallone movie where he put a gun to his side and shot bullets through himself to kill Antonio Banderas. That shit was awesome. It didn't even look like it hurt him at all. That's how you can tell someone is a real badass. They fucking shoot themselves and then act like they don't give a shit. Now, I've been in a lot of scrapes in my life, so I know that I'm pretty much a badass. I can take a punch. I've taken a lot. Most of the time I don't even cry. It's time to test my mettle. I'm going to shoot myself and kill a fake cop in the process. Yes indeedy, being a cop is totally fucking awesome. If shit like this happens to cops every day, then you can sign my ass up for the academy.

"I have identification."

"Keep your hands on your head!"

"You will be sorry when you find out who you're arresting. I *know* people." My words weren't doing anything to get the cop to allow me to move. It probably didn't help that a man that I just judged is hanging by his neck and choking with his leg half chewed off. I was starting to feel a little down, when I had an epiphany. I am not the one who should be afraid. Cops are supposed to stand up to danger with bravery. I am not some namby-pamby fraidy cat. I am a fucking badass and this joker is fucking toast.

"I'm going to take my hands off my head and turn around."

"You fucking turn around and I'm going to blow your head off!"

"I am a cop."

"You are not a cop. Shut the fuck up and don't move."

"I'm moving."

I drop my hands and hear a shot. I wait for the bullet to strike me, but I don't feel it. I'm pretty sure that I am in some kind of shock so I look down and check myself. No blood and no pain. Either I haven't been shot or shock is pretty fucking awesome.

"Don't turn around."

What the fuck is it with people not wanting me to turn around? Baltimore is a pretty fucked up place if people don't want other people to look at them. What the fuck? The voice is different and this dude isn't yelling at me anymore.

"Did you shot the cop?"

"I did. What the fuck did you do to my friend?"

"I'm a cop."

"Fat fucking chance."

"He was breaking the law. I sentenced him to death."

"Sorry to tell you. You're the one that's going to die."

I take the gun out of my belt and slowly put the barrel against my stomach a little off to the right. Right where I watched Sly Stallone do his shit in the movie.

"Are you ready to die?"

I imagined the man talking to me in the silky tones of Banderas. I responded like I had a mouth full of spit, shit, and marbles.

"You first, asshole."

I fired the gun into my stomach. The force of the bullet made me bend forward. Holy shit that shit hurt! What the fuck! Can't we trust movies anymore! Hollywood will be the recipient of another strongly worded letter. I have some fucking writing to do. Not right now though. Right now I'm fucking bleeding and my stomach hurts like hell.

"You just fucking shot yourself."

"I was trying to shoot you by shooting through my own stomach."

"Like that *Assassins* movie?"

"Exactly."

"I love that fucking movie."

I turned my head and saw this huge white guy wearing jeans and a wife-beater shirt. He had an old looking 9mm handgun in his hand. I looked down at the body on the floor. That fucker wasn't wearing a clown suit at all. That was a fucking cop and that cop was fucking dead.

"I think I'm dying."

"Probably not. You won't die for a while at least."

"Did I shoot you? Did it work?"

"Nope. You just shot yourself. Movies are all full of shit."

"Tell me about it."

I sat up and put a hand on my stomach. Bringing it away showed a wide swath of blood on my hand.

"You still going to shoot me?"

"No. that guy behind you wasn't really my friend. I was actually coming to kill him."

He raised the gun and shot the hanging man several times. The man gurgled as blood began to pour from his mouth. His body jerked a couple times and then stopped. Justice had been served. To be truthful, I was a little pissed off that the guy was the one to serve justice. When a cop kills someone – it's justice. When someone else does it – it's murder. I was going to look the other way on this one, but just this once.

"What are you going to do with me?"

"Did you chew that guy's leg off?"

"Just a bit."

"You do this messy type of shit a lot?"

"It's growing on me."

"Come on. I have something to do and I think you are the perfect person to take with me. We'll go to the clinic first. Lots of people are getting shot in Baltimore these days. They won't think a thing of digging that slug out of you."

I was totally fucking game. Especially for the whole 'getting the bullet out of me' part.

"Let's go."

IT TURNS OUT THAT THE 'TAKING THE BULLET OUT OF ME PART' REALLY SUCKED. That fucker was really deep inside of me and the dude didn't take me to the clinic like he said. This one dude who said he was a nurse or something just kind of dug into me and took out the lead. I don't think that dude was a nurse. It's not like I could do anything about it. The fucker had me tied up first. There wasn't anything I could do about that. I was in too much pain to fight them off. I guess it serves me right for plugging myself in the stomach. I was lying on some shitty bed with linens that smelled like sweat and rancid food when the guy comes in. He doesn't even ask me how I'm doing.

"We leave tonight. You should be okay by then."

"Where are we going?"

"You're going to dress up in your cop stuff and head downtown."

"I've already done that. You told me that I was in for some serious shit."

"You are. You're going to kill a bunch of cops."

Now this was something completely different. I've never been much for killing people, even though I've done that a few times. It doesn't really do anything for me. Killing cops was never on my radar as something that I wanted to do, but maybe this guy was on to something. Maybe I should have been killing cops all along. The guy was just fucking smiling down on me like he knew that I knew what he was thinking. We were on the same fucking wavelength. I fucking love rioting and I'm always looking for a better way to get off.

What's been keeping me down is really just the fucking cops. People are always shitty about cops, but they are always calling them when they get into trouble. They hate cops until they fucking need them, then they love the fuckers. The cops are like the fourth wall. People get all riled up and shit, and they let loose, but the cops are always pulling them back from the big blastoff. Get the fucking cops out of the way and you'll have total anarchy. This was a fucking awesome idea! I don't know why the fuck I didn't think about it before. I went in looking to get off at a riot by being a cop, but the real juice is getting rid of the cops so you can riot to the fucking maximum extreme. I don't even know what rioting to the maximum extreme means, I just want to fucking do it. If I kill a couple of cops, then the people will follow and we will run over the law like a fucking tidal wave. Then we can do whatever the fuck we want. We're going to light the fires until the whole fucking state burns to the ground. I could give a fuck less if Baltimore burns to the ground. I live in fucking Missouri. Baltimore can be wiped off the fucking map for all I care.

"This is a fucking great idea."

"I know. Do you think you'll be ready by tonight?"

"My stomach really fucking hurts, but I should be okay, I think."

"Awesome. I've got some stuff I have to do to get ready. I'll see you later. Rest up."

"Fucking A."

IT TURNS OUT THAT KILLING COPS IS A LOT HARDER THAN I WOULD HAVE FIRST THOUGHT. First of all, those fuckers are in some pretty serious armor. The shot has to be fucking perfect. Right in the fucking neck. Sure cops were getting wounded all over the place. Tons of shit had been written about taxpayer cost for the cops who had to go on light duty or medical leave to nurse their injuries from the riots. That's all well and fine for them, but I had some fucking killing to do. I was thinking of point blank shooting the cops in the neck like I just said a bit ago. This would work, but then I had to rely on the people to start bowling them over and going apeshit right away. If they hesitated then I was fucked for sure. The other problem that I had was that I was getting a bit of a liking for police work. It wasn't as good a buzz as rioting, but it got me off okay. If I liken the two to having dinner, then rioting would be the steak, being a cop would be the mashed potato side dish. As much as I like rioting, I realize that it doesn't happen all the time, and most of the time I have to travel to do it. Police officers are everywhere all the time. I could do the cop thing twenty four seven if I wanted to. Going back to the restaurant dinner metaphor – you don't always get steak, but fucking potatoes are always there. Potatoes are cheap and are a fucking staple. Steak is for the better times. Fucking rich people food and shit.

I had all my gear on and the guy gave me a couple of extra 9mm guns. I don't know how many cops they expected me to be able to kill. I was thinking maybe I would get one, but I had enough bullets to take out a whole line. Maybe they just think I'm a shit shot with the damn things. They would be right. I don't get much practice with guns, but I know which end fires and when the muzzle is touching neck flesh you don't have to be a good shot at all.

It took me a little longer to get into the middle of the shit. The guy told me that he would have people getting the public all rowdied up for when I started taking the cops down. I couldn't help but be late. There was many a nefarious deed going on that I had to do a lot of cop shit on my way to the riots. Many people got busted, figuratively and literally. Being a cop was a lot of work. Fun though. By the time I was finished my right pants pocket was half full of teeth. I thought about making a necklace out of them when this was all over. Baltimore was off the fucking chain (to use the black way of saying something was fucking awesome). I needed a memento to remember this by when things got peaceful.

The cops didn't stop me from getting into the line. I was put in the second row. I didn't look much like them. My shield was gone and I didn't have the vest they were all wearing. They looked like they were from the movie universal soldier or some shit. The good thing was that I had a lot of blood on me and my helmet was well dented, I think they thought I came from some other part of the rioting that was a lot worse than the shit they were dealing with. They asked me if I was hurt. I told them that the blood wasn't mine and that I was really happy to see them. They grabbed me and put me behind the first line. They looked like the Spartan 300 of the future. They were all lined up, shields together, and nothing but armor. It was nice of the police to keep me away from the front line, because those people were really fucking angry and throwing shit and going after the police. They weren't just rioting, stealing and breaking shit. They were fucking mad. It looked like they were all about to run over the cops no matter what I did. This was good, because I was totally fucking freaked out. The other part of me was pretty pissed that I was in the second line. I looked really fucked up, and a lot of the people behind me barely had dust on their uniforms. Why the shit was I supposed to be in the second line, backing up the first? I should have been given a break. Maybe coffee and a donut or something. I don't know what the cops do, but this was some bullshit.

Part of my problem was that I was seeing a lot of action in the second line. The rioters were in full swing. The police was trying to take the street, but we were at a fucking standstill with the people. They weren't fucking moving back an inch, let alone dispersing like a couple cops talking into bullhorns told them too. We were fucking stuck. They were battling the cops in front, not very well, but they were attacking pretty hard. The cops were pushing them back, trying not to get too physical with them. I guess the cops were still afraid that they would get into trouble. I didn't feel this way.

"You will obey the law!" I shouted and swung hard with my baton. My shot went between the heads of two cops in front of me and brained some chick that was pressing up against the police line. At first I thought that I was going to get into trouble, but the cops didn't say shit. They even stepped forward a couple of paces, stepping on and over the woman I just smashed. The cops behind me picked her up and tossed her in a paddy wagon. She was under arrest! By me! I started to realize that I was the best police officer in the world. These guys didn't know shit about what they were doing and I was about to teach them. Every minute or so I would swing forward and nail a rioter. I was getting so into it that I would use the cops' shoulders in front of me as leverage to jump up and swing further into the crowd. I was hitting with every swing. The people couldn't very well move back. There were pressed with the rowdies from behind. Whenever I took a person down, the line moved to take up that space. This was fucking awesome.

My arm started to hurt from all the beatings I was dishing out. I started to think about my insurance plan. I assumed that cops had a pretty fucking good one. I hoped it covered carpal tunnel syndrome. I guess I didn't think a person could get that unless they typed on a keyboard all day, but smashing shitheads using the same hand and arm motion over and over could cause the same thing. The police had better cover my medical bills. This is a risky job.

I was bashing the fuck out of people when I realized that I actually needed these people whole. I had forgotten that I was supposed to be taking out the cops and releasing the beast of the populace. What I was doing did have a desired effect though. The people were pissed off before I got there. When they witnessed what I was doing they reached a higher level of pissed off-edness that I had never thought possible. They started launching at the police line, specifically where I was, to try and take me down. Maybe I was thinning the herd a little bit too much, but the fuckers that I left standing were really fucking pissed off. I knew that this was the time to act.

I drew the 9mm I had tucked into my belt. Before I could get a shot off, a cop grabbed my arm from behind.

"Don't fucking do it. I know you want too. I want to do it too, but you have to lay off. I've been watching you. Don't lose it."

This fucker has had eyes on me this whole time that I'd been slamming people. I thought that I was scot free with the bullshit I'd been up to, but this guy was watching me and only letting me do what I wanted to because he wanted to get off like I was. In short, this guy had no balls of his own and wanted to borrow mine. There was a line that I was about to cross, in his mind, where he didn't want to handle my balls at all. He didn't want me to shoot the people. He might have been watching me, but he was dead wrong about my intentions with the gun. I lowered the gun a bit to show that I was compliant with what he wanted me to do. He loosened his grip on my arm and patted me on the shoulder.

I put the gun under his chin and pulled the trigger.

His helmet visor went red immediately. Blood and brain matter poured out through the hole in his chin. I turned around and shot the cop in front of me and a bit to my left under his jawline. He dropped. I quickly shot the cop next to him through the neck. They dropped, but not before the second cop grabbed me and pulled me down with him. I heard gunfire from behind me. The cops had opened fire on me, but those fuckers missed. The bullets all went into the armor of the dead cop that I had just shot. Thank fuck that I landed under the guy. The cops that were shooting at me accidently killed a few civilians with their stray bullets. This was just the shit that I needed.

The line of cops lost their discipline as soon as I killed their fellows. Some of them acted murderously, for sure, but others just fucking froze, unsure of what to do. This was just long enough for the people to catch them off guard and start breaking their line with a fury of rocks, slamming bodies and even a nice amount of gunfire from whatever shit they brought from home. If you know America at all, you know that most homes have a gun; lots of them have a fucking armory.

I was fucking laughing until the people turned their shit on me.

IT'S A SHITTY THING TO MISS THE GREATEST RIOT IN THE HISTORY OF AMERICA. Especially for a person like me. I travel halfway across the country to get in on the action and the action happened without me. Well, technically I *was* there. I was just unconscious for most of it. I'm sure those asshole civilians saw me shoot those fucking cops. It was obvious that I was a double agent, or triple reverse agent, or something. It doesn't matter. I was the one who shot those cops and gave the people the window they needed to reach total anarchy. I was the one who made the shit hit the fan. I am a man of history. At least I'm not in jail or dead. Either of which I was expecting after the people starting beating me up.

I've never felt anything like it. They ran over me like a wave, clawing, kicking, and tearing at me. I lost my helmet and my armor. People punched and kicked me in the face, ribs, and groin. I was one hot searing fireball of pain when I lost consciousness. Thank goodness for that. I'm so pissed off that I missed the anarchy, but what did I expect really? It was anarchy. What did I want, controlled anarchy? That shit doesn't exist.

I can't really tell why I wasn't arrested. I think it was because I was stripped of my cop shit and most of my clothes. With all that shit gone, I expect I just looked like another douche bag victim of all the shit that's been going down. There are bodies all around me. The air is filled with smoke. Buildings are burning all around. There are ambulances, cops, firefighters, and civilians helping the hurt people and trying to put out fires, but there aren't enough of them to make any difference. Shit is really fucked up. All these bodies lying around me won't be moved for a long time. I see cops, black people, white people, and the occasional Hispanic. I don't see any Asians, but that's not a surprise. Asians don't fall for this kind of shit. It's a shame that anarchy is what it took to bring the races and people of different walks of life together. That and death, I guess. When you die you don't really get to pick where your body falls.

From the looks of things, I'm pretty lucky to be alive. It feels pretty good too. I've always heard about people who've had near death experiences being all happy and shit. Damn, those fuckers were right. If I had died then I wouldn't be able to riot again and that would be some bullshit. I know that most people who almost die come back and turn their personalities over, feed the poor, plant trees and all that shit. Not fucking me. I'm glad I'm alive so I can get my rocks off again. Can't do that shit when you're worm food. Fuck that.

I'm too fucked up to really do anything. I have no fucking money to go to the hospital. I'm going to find my fucking car and drive the fuck home. I don't care what's going on here. I don't care how many people are dead. I don't care that I'm violating the oath I took as a fake policeman. Fuck Baltimore. Fuck it right in the face.

HERE'S THE FUCKING THING. People don't give a shit about each other. Sometimes they come together singing 'Hands Across America' or some kind of other happy shit, but that's all bullshit. People come together to dogpile on other people. Most conversations people have with others are about tearing down other people or systems. Not many people give back to this world more than they take from it. The people that do? You can't trust those fuckers. They are more than likely hiding some pretty awful shit that they're making up for.

People in this world are in it for themselves. That's the bottom fucking line. The bottom of the bottom of the fucking line is that people feel at their best when they tear the bottom line out from others. That's where the real fucking juice is. People fuck each other around every single fucking day and they are horrible to their fucking heroes. If someone looks up to you, you better watch their fucking back because they are going to get a real good jerk-off session when you fall down. People love that shit.

I'm not saying that I'm above any of that shit. You've read this and it's pretty apparent that I couldn't really give a fuck about my neighbor, but at least I'm fucking honest about. Unlike everyone else. I just really don't give a shit about people. I rioted as a black person, a white person, a cop, and a cop killer. I got off and it was fucking great. I got mine. Fuck you.

Let me tell you something I've come to understand about rioting. People don't riot for a cause. People riot because they want to destroy. There's no other meaning to it. People just want to fuck shit up. It's natural. If you want to stop people from rioting, then you should just shoot the fuckers that do it and then you won't have the problem anymore. It's an easy answer. If I was shot and killed then I wouldn't be fucking rioting anymore, now would I? Fuck no.

The only reason that rioters aren't shot and killed on sight is that more people aren't into that kind of thing than are. If the majority was for plugging rioters, then it would be open fucking season. This is the way the world works. Don't give me any shit about America being a civilized society and that's why we don't do that kind of shit. Civilized societies do all sorts of rotten shit. Just because we're supposed to live under a certain moral code doesn't enter into anything. It's just the way the majority wants things. They have other ways they like to get off and that's okay. They look down on rioting, but at least I know that here I won't get killed for it. If I started this kind of shit in China or something, my ass would have been plugged for sure.

The fucking Chinese don't mess around with that kind of shit.

I know that this shit is done for me for a while. At least in Baltimore anyway. When you kill a bunch of cops and cause all sorts of mayhem, then you have to lay low for a bit. I won't be down forever. There will be other riots. People are always starting all sorts of shit. Maybe I'll put aside some money every paycheck so I can have a little nest egg in case the shit hits the fan in another country. I would like to check out a French riot sometime. We'll just have to see.

I need to get off. You need to get off. We all fucking need to get off. My fucking balls are drained for now, but they get plumper every day.

Every fucking day.

Dictated but not read,

Blackface Rioter.

<u>*MorbidbookS*</u> *Is A Grotesque Bizarro Ballet Where The Most Profane Things Occur. An Impious And Perverse Dwelling Of Dark Revulsion. A Cozy Cottage Where Torture Porn And Brutal Bible Tales Are Devised. A Quiet Place To Relax And Spin Tales Of Depravity And Wickedness. A Halfway House For The Disturbed Where Rules No Longer Apply. A Safe Haven For Deviant Serial Killers To Hatch Their Wretched Schemes. Bring Your Pets. The Tasty Ones Are Always Welcome.*

Also available from ~MorbidbookS~

In Print & Kindle Editions. Available at Amazon.com,

CreateSpace.com, and Barnes&Noble stores & online.

~click on Kindle image for HYPERLINK~

~Maybe it had started when he was at university.

He had a girlfriend in his final year that had gotten him into some weird stuff sexually then she left him for a guy with a bigger cock. The other guy was some gay looking chump with muscles and a tattoo; the pair had died in a car accident and Brian took a dump on their graves after each of their funerals. Fuck the both of them. But after she had left him he needed to fill the void of the newfound enjoyment of sickening sexual practices. Brain had purchased one of those 'real life' sex dolls online. Boy did the thing look real; you could bend it into any position and it came armed with enormous tits, willing mouth and a supposedly real feel pussy and anus. The packaging said to 'just add lubricant' but there was a problem. There was something missing; the smells, the tastes and the feel of real skin. You can't emulate that. So Brian set out to attempt to build a real life sex toy made from real life people.

~**Keegan is a late-night public access radio show host,** sexual deviant, and militant vegan. He has grown tired of his vegan cause being treated with apathy by the portly, meat-gorging, residents of the small town of Breen Gay, Wisconsin.

The time is ripe for Vegan vengeance.

Keegan harvests roundworms from a local vagrant and mutates them using chemicals stolen from the meat packing plant. He infests the populace with the voracious, parasitic carnivores. Keegan knows that the only way for the people of Breen Gay to eliminate the parasites is to starve them of meat. It is with great expectation that he awaits the oncoming utopia of Veganism.

However, the mutant roundworms will not die easily. The problems for the people of Breen Gay have only just begun.

~**FOR SO LONG as anyone could remember,** The Flagrant Five have ruled the land with an aggressive hand—enslaving children, destroying the wilderness—but Father Necrocious is tired of it all. One of his worst enemies (and a member of the Flagrant Five), Manservant Genesis, has escaped his imprisonment as a shadow. Therefore, he's enlisted the help of a ragtag group of fabricated Mercenaries to turn the fascists to shadows. The annual Dictators' Ball is pending (a battle in which children are used as pawns to determine the fate of the free world), and the brothers plan to stop the gala before it can commence. As they weave their way through the cartoonish landscape they will fight with their options to either trap the Flagrant Five with their shadow guns, or disobey their creator's orders and finally kill the Five for good.

~The hands of the girls were inside of each-others zip front grey boiler suits and they sat in the blood from where Sonny's face collided with the surface. The brunette had a finger smear of it next to her mouth.

"You two sluts put each other down and go tell Moira that Sonny's done. I'm coming in, just got a little business to attend to first."

As the two started to leave the big blond grabbed the shoulder of the red head and pulled her back.

"Not you Fire-Crotch, all this fucking blood has got me going."

She started to unbuckle the belt on her camouflage hot pants.

"Down you go, bitch!"

~**Short stories from the Most Depraved Writer in Print.** Dark and twisted tales of exquisite violence, rough tricks, narcotics consumption, evil ghosts and drug-snuffling demons. Evil grandfathers and animal–human hybrid clones. Morbid serial killer stalking night darkened hallways of an unsuspecting hospital. Life underground following the frozen apocalypse. Tales of ancient blood–thirsty vampires and Roman decadence. Enjoy all of the hardcore, dystopic, viscerally violent stories. Not for easily offended mamby–pambies. Dark fiction at its finest.

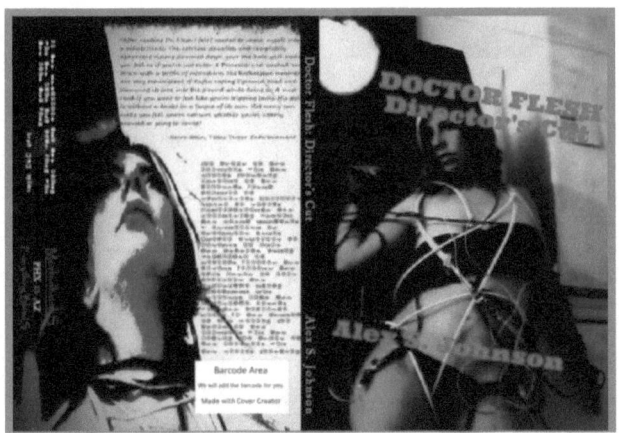

~From Alex S. Johnson, the author of **Bad Sunset, Wicked Candy and The Death Jazz,** comes a new vision in Bizarro horror. Imagine a TROMA film on meth and acid, one part cyberpunk, one part Franz Kafka, and three parts frankly unsuitable for a sane audience. "Will make you feel as if you've just eaten 8 Percocets and washed 'em down with a bottle of moonshine," says Necro Stein of Texas Terror Entertainment.

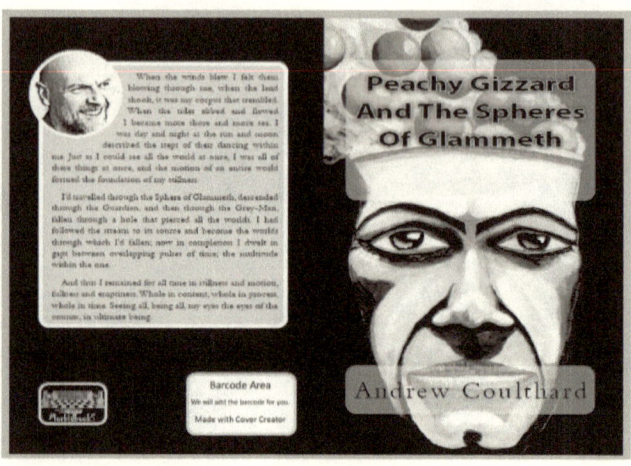

~**When the winds blew i felt them blowing through me,** when the land shook, it was my corpus that trembled. When the tides ebbed and flowed I became more shore and more sea. I was day and night as the sun and moon described the steps of their dancing within me. Just as I could see all the world at once, I was all of these things at once, and the motion of an entire world formed the foundation of my stillness.

I'd travelled through the Sphere of Glammeth, descended through the Guardian, and then through the Grey-Man, fallen through a hole that pierced all the worlds.

~**He had to have her the moment he saw her trachea ring.** Six months later she was his lovely wife. He performed his duties as a husband and she as a wife. He tolerated a house filled with references to her late first husband and the children they had together. He put up with her prudish ways. He waited. He was patient. He planned. He was adaptable. He was rewarded over the course of a week in her basement. He turned his perverse sexual fantasies of worms and maggots and her lovely crusty trachea ring into a gruesome reality.

~A dirty shameful devil of a secret...

Something that two men share. A legacy that will shock you to your very core. One that is created not out of madness, but of the purest desire. Take a vivid journey into the mind of the killer and his biggest fan. Do you believe in evil? See the knife plunge. Lap at the wounds. Do you still? There is no rational meaning or pretty words that will hide away the darkness that the words of this found journal creates. Inside is the real truth. And it can set you free. Watch all you want. Taste what you dare not have.

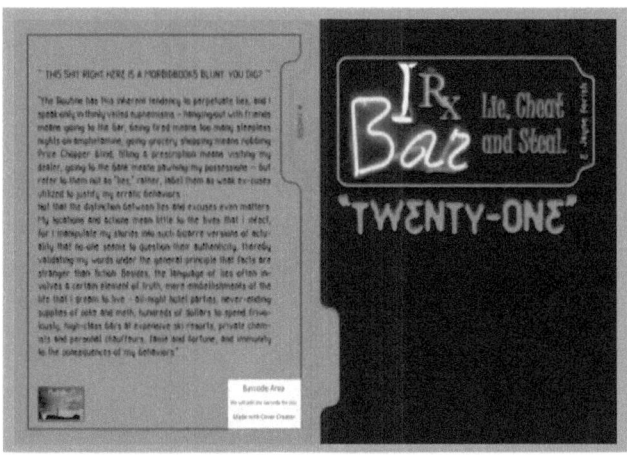

~"The routine has this inherent tendency to perpetuate lies, and I speak only in thinly veiled euphemisms — hanging out with friends means going to the bar; being tired means too many sleepless nights on amphetamine; going grocery shopping means robbing Price Chopper blind; filling a prescription means visiting my dealer; going to the bank means pawning my possessions — but refer to them not as "lies;" rather, label them as weak excuses utilized to justify my erratic behaviours.

~**I'm feeling down and dirty, feeling kind of mean,** so I give those fans my middle finger. Those poor bastards go nuts. My team looks at me in awe. My coach frowns and the opposing one begins to furiously scratch out new plays. I see our opponents and I almost feel sorry for the poor bastards. Their fans can't help them. Their coach can't help them. I'm going to run them off their own track in front of their own fans and there is not one thing they can do about it.

~**Humanity is the devil is a deconstructed nightmare mixing David Lynch and snuff movies.** The plot revolves around a central character, Seth, who is set about a crusade against humanity which, for him, represents pure evil. Through random killings he and his cronies try to accelerate the end of the world, in order to provoke and defeat the Demiurge, the false God that is ruling the earth. As in Burroughs, logical language is replaced here with cut-scenes – sometimes to be taken literally   that plunge the reader into an extreme experience.

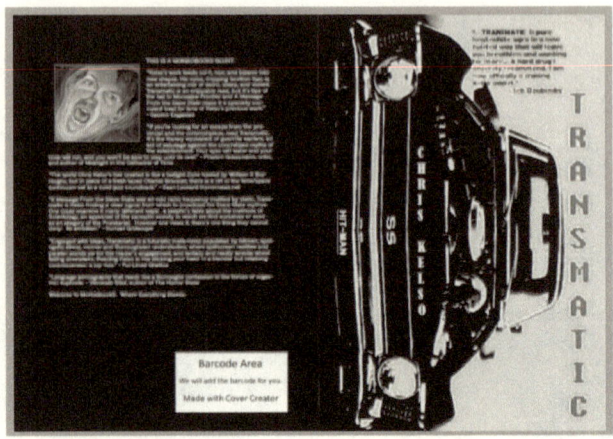

~"As a part-time hitman/ exterminator, Ignius Ellis's dream is to buy a candy-apple red Nova Supreme. In the process of trying to earn enough cash to make his dream come true he gets sucked into the rough world of Visitacion Valley, SF. When the tenants in his apartment complex reveal their various extracurricular activities this take an even more bizarre twist and Ellis soon becomes acquainted with the nightmarish Slave State dimension..."

~That's the last time she gets the bigger worm...

Once their flesh flakes away the angels collapse into puddles of hissing goop and withered petals blow into them hurried along by unseen winds. My spit looses its sweet taste to the black flavor of ash. The glowing birds in the bright orange sky burst into small sparkly novas. The sky itself weeps and tears, streaking down like a ruined painting as the dismal grey of life wheezes back before my eyes. I don't blink; praying silently for one last desperate sensation of the high. Lila feels it too. She writhes on the mattress next to me...

~**Within these twisted and perverted pages**, Johnson manages to demolish clichés with a jaded finesse that I've personally never encountered in written form. Another apparent talent is his effortless deconstruction of pop-culture allegories and references as found in his story "Vampussy." No one is safe or spared from his dagger sharp sarcasm and wit.

While not without its flaws, my appreciation for this kind of talent and voice is what made his writing so fun to read, even if he might possibly be out of his ever-loving mind.

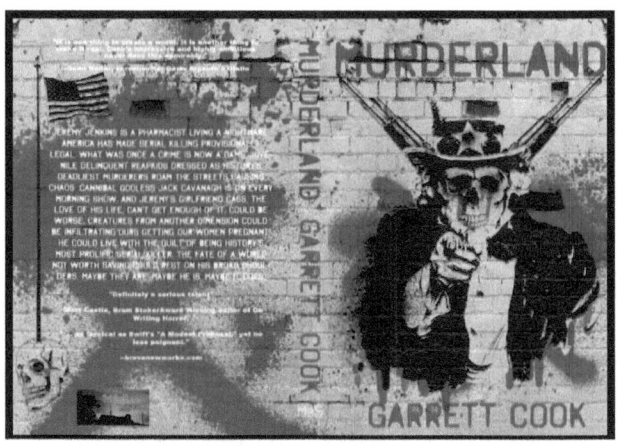

~In Garrett Cook's Murderland serial killers are idolized by society. Their deeds are followed obsessively by television pundits and the adoring public. A subculture has grown up around this phenomena, called "Reap." Laws are created to allow this activity to flourish, including designated "safe zones' where killers can practice their trade without fear of persecution. Fans of the top rated serial killers celebrate each new kill on social media and television. Programs glorify their deeds.

The culture of Murderland is violent and mirrors our own violent society and its decadent obsessions.

~**Born whole from the rectum of a dying patient, Morbid silently stalks the hospital's hallways,** heinously dispatching the most helpless of patients and in the most painfully repulsive of manners. In the meantime, in order to pay for his family and home that includes his ghost step-father Sammy and his pet aborted fetus Chip, Westphal has to ingest mounds of dangerous narcotics to get through his night shifts. Barely hanging on to his Care Tech gig by his fingernails, the last thing Westphal needs is to be accused of Morbid's evil deeds. You, on the other hand, simply seek some solace from all Your diseases.

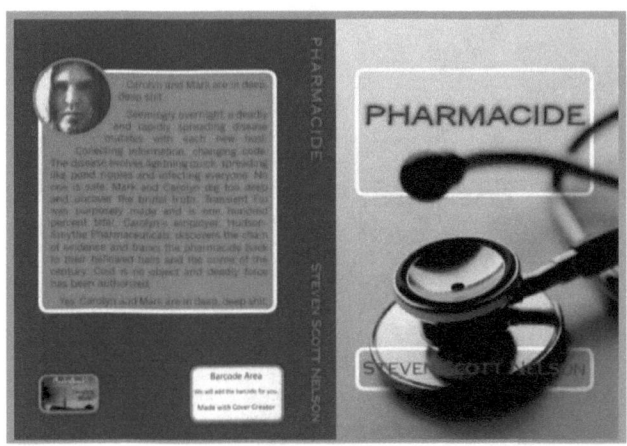

~It looks like Carolyn and Mark are in deep, deep shit... Mark and Carolyn live in an alternate 1989 where Ronald Reagan is on his fourth presidential term. The USA has a rigid, long-standing caste system and abortions were never made legal. Being homeless is a crime that is punishable by imprisonment in Tent City. Most of Mark's ER patients are inmates at this camp and are victims of a new disease dubbed: Transient Flu. This deadly and rapidly spreading disease mutates with each new host, collecting information, changing code. The disease evolves lightning quick, spreading like pond ripples...

~IMMANUEL THE CHRIST has some nerve. Jonah has already lost everyone he loves to Pilate the vampire and his Harbor drug violence. Jonah now trudges through his days staying as high on Plata as possible. He just wants to be left alone while he waits for his turn to die. The Christ has other plans for him. She sends Pedro, to assign Jonah to order the Herod to dismantle the Harbor's Plata trade. Jonah decides to run. But you can't run from God. As Jonah learns the hard way when the 'Edmund Fitzgerald' goes down in rough seas, with the reluctant prophet on board…

~**Five Very Wicked Shorts**. Brought to you with love and blood from The Grim Reverend Steven Rage, the 'Most Depraved Writer in Print'. ~

Through the sheer shock of his presentation, Rage forces readers to consider the alternatives, to look at the garbage in the streets, to see what is swept into the gutters at night right before all decent people awake to see another cleaned up version of the day. Depravity at its finest, but really the stories are loads of fun.

~Pontius Pilate is cursed to be a vampire. Life after life after life.~ And for the Plata dealing Pilate, his life is more like a death sentence. His only chance surviving is to keep on selling his monthly quota of Plata. This new man-made narcotic is a potent speed-ball designed to amp up the user, while also numbing the conscience into euphoric oblivion. To nullify the pain. To stifle the torture. To run and to hid from all the anguish inside. PILATE is a drug lord vampire in this re-telling of Christ's final days.

~**Following religious folklore, parables, and beliefs,** Rage presents the readers with a God who truly is the Shepherd that leaves no sheep behind. While this tale is deeply woven with the intricacies of a dark, drug-infested world ruled by evil forces, this is the story of a lost sheep. All are God's children, even the most foulest of evil creatures who by their own will have become so through their spiritual and physical copulation with the Devil, and as such, in God's mercy, still are given a chance to be saved.

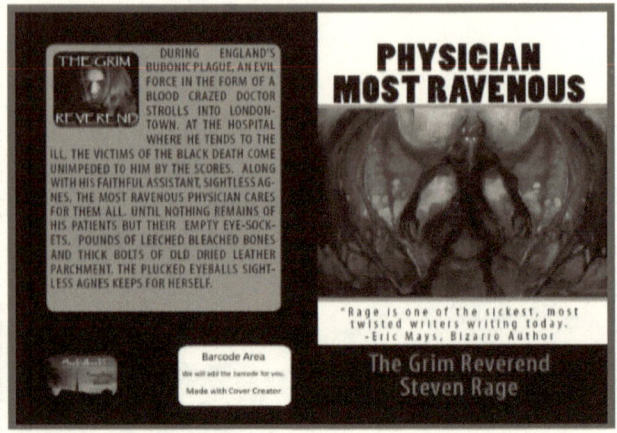

~During the height of England's Bubonic Plague an ancient Evil Force strolls into London-Town in the form of a would-be doctor. It could smell the blood from miles away, wanting only to help. At the hospital where he cares for the victims of this Black Death, the ill come to him unimpeded. They arrived and fell by the scores. With the help of his ever-faithful assistant, Sightless Agnes, a most ravenous cares for them all. Eating his way through an entire hospital, he treats them until there is nothing left. Nothing save their empty eye sockets, a few pounds of leeched bleached bones and some bolts of old dried-out flesh-leather parchment.

~New from MorbidbookS: Where Everything Bleeds is an instant collector's specimen and a certain stunner. ~ Be the first freak on your block to acquire this singular and unexpurgated exquisite culling of The Grim Reverend Steven Rage's favourite 'meds'. Enjoy this one-of-a-kind vivid look into the twisted mind of The Most Depraved Writer In Print as he captains you through the intoxicating stain of his wicked imagination. Included are numerous Photos, Paintings and Illustrations embellished with dramatic grayscale that enhance these iniquitous and magnificent Dark Fantasy fables.

"BURN, FERGUSON, BURN!"

~Click On Either Image For More from MorbidbookS On Kindle~

Morbidbook$
PHX~13~AZ
Everything Bleeds.

www.ingramcontent.com/pod-product-compliance
Lightning Source LLC
Chambersburg PA
CBHW021105130626
46554CB00002B/544